MW01615627

Daily Meditations for Lent 2025

Based on Catholic Mass Readings

Year I Cycle C

Rev. Charis Merced, PhD

Daily Meditations for Lent through Easter 2025: Based on Lectionary Readings
Copyright © 2024 by *Charis Merced, PhD*. All rights reserved.

No part of this book may be reproduced without written permission from the publisher or copyright holder, nor may any part of this book be stored or transmitted in any form or by any means, electronic, mechanical, photocopy, recording, or other, without prior written permission from the publisher or copyright holder. Unauthorized reproduction of this publication is prohibited.
All Scripture quotations are taken from **The New American Bible: St. Joseph Edition.** New York: Catholic Book Publishing Corp., 1991.
If you have enjoyed these meditations consider sharing a recommendation on Amazon.
Author's email is symeon.7.theologian@gmail.com
Author's address is Rev. Charis Merced P.O. Box 7, Clifford, PA. 18413-0007

Table of Contents

Introduction

"Then Jesus was led by the Spirit into the wilderness to be tempted by the devil. He fasted for forty days and forty nights"

(Matthew 4:1-2).

Each year, Christians are invited to journey with the Lord through a time of prayer, fasting, and reflection, just as He did during His 40 days in the wilderness. This sacred season, observed during Lent, calls us to prepare our hearts for the profound mysteries of Easter— Christ's suffering, death, and glorious resurrection. Lent is a time when both Catholic and Protestant believers are drawn into a deeper relationship with God, whether through attending church services, participating in a televised mass, or setting aside personal moments of prayer and meditation to walk in the footsteps of Jesus.

This book offers 47 daily meditations, beginning on Ash Wednesday and culminating on Easter Sunday. Each meditation is rooted in the mass readings of the day, with special emphasis on the Gospels. On Good Friday, we will contemplate the challenging subject of suicide, offering a space for solemn reflection. Holy Saturday's meditation invites us to journey through the story of salvation—from creation to resurrection—as we prepare for the dawn of new life in Christ.

If these meditations touch your heart, provide comfort, or spark inspiration, I kindly encourage you to share your experience by leaving a review on Amazon. Also, keep an eye out for our Advent meditations, as we continue to seek God's presence throughout all sacred seasons.

May God's abundant blessings be with you,

Rev. Charis Merced, PhD

Day 1
Ash Wednesday

March 5, 2025

Isaiah 58:1–12

Psalm 51:1–17

2 Cor. 5:20b–6:10

Matthew 6:1–6;16–21

"[But] take care not to perform righteous deeds in order that people may see them; otherwise, you will have no recompense from your heavenly Father."

(Matthew 6:1)

If the first question you ask is, "What do I have to do for Lent?" you might be missing a profound opportunity. This question can suggest that whatever you undertake is being imposed as an obligation. But when gratitude is forced, like when someone is made to say "Thank you," the words and effort often feel hollow to both the giver and the receiver. We must remember that all our blessings come from God, and among the greatest of these is the gift of His Son, Jesus Christ. His sacrifice on the Cross opened the gates of heaven for us. True gratitude says, "Thank You, Lord! Let me show You how deeply I appreciate Your blessings by doing X, Y, and Z." The motivation for a

1

spiritual life should never be obligation; it should spring from a heart overflowing with thankfulness. As William Arthur Ward wisely said, "Gratitude can transform common days into thanksgivings, turn routine jobs into joy, and change ordinary opportunities into blessings." God pours blessings upon us for one reason alone: because God is love. Lent, then, is our communal response to God's abundant blessings. Lent does not change God, but it has the power to change us.

Gratitude is often called the mother of all virtues, and it is a fundamental prerequisite for genuine religion. Without gratitude, religion becomes hollow, and worship loses its substance. Every blessing we receive is a personal and intentional gift from a loving Creator. This understanding is where the three pillars of Jewish piety—prayer, almsgiving, and fasting—come into play, for each pillar is a response to God's benevolent gifts.

Jesus expressed His gratitude to the Creator through His life of prayer, His acts of giving to the poor, and His practice of fasting. Sacrificial worship involves surrendering something to God as an expression of deep gratitude. Prayer offers up our time, our words, and our praise to the Father. Almsgiving and acts of mercy transform our interactions with others into moments of worship, where our brothers and sisters become the altars upon which we serve and honor God. As Jesus said, *"Whatever you did for one of these least brothers of mine, you did for me"* (Matthew 25:40). Fasting

2

sharpens our awareness of the One who provides our daily bread. Notice how Jesus doesn't say "if you fast," but rather, "when you fast" (Matthew 6:17). This assumption speaks to the heart of our spiritual journey: the goal is to establish deep communion with God and one another, and the path to that communion is paved with gratitude.

God's gifts are more numerous than the grains of sand on the earth's shores—food and clothing, loved ones, health, the beauty of the night sky, faith in Jesus, a place to call home, and even the very breath of life itself. Each of these must be recognized and returned to the Giver in acts of praise. We come into this world with nothing, and we leave with nothing. Blessed be the Lord! As Melody Beattie eloquently put it, "Gratitude unlocks the fullness of life. It turns what we have into enough, and more. It turns denial into acceptance, chaos to order, confusion to clarity."

As we embark on our Lenten journey, let gratitude be the guiding light that leads us closer to God. But let's not stop at words—let our gratitude be evident in our actions, in the sacrifices we make, in the prayers we offer, and in the love we share with others. Surrender something to God this Lent as an act of sacrificial worship through prayer, almsgiving, and fasting. Let us begin this sacred journey with hearts full of thanks and a sincere commitment to follow His will. As we walk this path together, let our prayer be, "*Here I am, Lord; I come to do Your will"*(Hebrews 10:9). And may this Lent be a time of deep renewal, drawing us ever closer to the heart of God, where we find our true peace, purpose, and joy.

Lenten Reflection: The best way to begin Lent might be to make a list of your blessings and add to it as you move through these next forty-seven days. Those blessings are not accidents but intentionally chosen for you by God. All religion begins with gratitude.

Day 2

Thursday after Ash Wednesday

March 6, 2025

Deuteronomy 30:15–20

Psalm 1:1–2, 3, 4, 6

Luke 9:22–25

"If anyone wishes to come after me, he must deny himself and take up his cross daily and follow me."

(Luke 9:23)

Moses and Jesus, both present us with a profound choice in our Bible readings today: to love God and keep His commandments or to face spiritual death. The life Moses speaks of is centered on earthly blessings—having children, enjoying bountiful harvests, and living in times of peace. It is a life defined by the tangible rewards of faithfulness here on earth. But the life Jesus offers reaches far beyond the temporal; it extends into the eternal. He promises us immortality, a life that transcends this world and continues forever in the presence of God.

However, neither Moses nor Jesus promises an easy path to this inheritance. Jesus, in particular, makes it clear that the journey He sets before us is one marked by sacrifice, suffering, forgiveness, and the inevitable cross we must bear. There is no Christianity without the cross. Crucifixion, in a metaphorical sense, is a part of the journey each believer must face. Just as the repeated strikes of Michelangelo's hammer against the marble revealed the beauty of the Pietà, so too does God use the trials of life to shape and refine our souls. How can the final version of your soul be revealed without the hammer and chisel of divine craftsmanship?

A life filled only with abundance, answered prayers, love, and affection often leads to shallow, selfish, and entitled souls—souls lacking the depth needed for empathy, compassion, or self-sacrifice. It is through tears that the cataracts of self-sufficiency are removed, allowing us to see the world and our fellow humans as they truly are. Without suffering, we risk becoming helpless adults, unable to face the challenges of life. In fact, modern psychology describes this condition as "learned helplessness," a state where individuals feel powerless to change their circumstances.

If you desire something truly precious, like diamonds or gold, you must be willing to dig deep into the mine. The cost is high—it involves pick and shovel, blistered hands, and even blackened lungs. Similarly, we are given the raw clay of our souls, and God calls us to work diligently, to get our hands calloused and our fingers burned as we shape ourselves on the potter's wheel and fire our hearts in the kiln of life's trials.

To expect a meaningful life without the reality of crucifixion is delusional. Crucifixion is not an option we can choose to bypass; it is a certainty we must face. The only question that remains is how we will respond when suffering inevitably comes. Will you pick up your cross and move forward, one arduous, painful step at a time, with your heart and eyes focused on Jesus? Will you try to walk around the cross, pretending it's not there, or will you deny its existence altogether, keeping your head in the clouds and a superficial smile on your face?

Every truly precious thing in this world comes at a high price. Jesus is offering us the ultimate treasure—a seat at the table with His Father and the Holy Spirit. Such a priceless gift is worth any sacrifice. Why would we expect the tickets to this eternal feast to be free?

As we reflect on the choices before us, let us remember that the road to true life is often paved with challenges and trials. Yet, it is through these very challenges that we are shaped into the people God calls us to be. Embrace your cross with courage and hope, knowing that each step you take brings you closer to the fullness of life that Jesus promises. In the end, the sacrifices we make and the crosses we bear will lead us to a glory that far surpasses anything this world can offer. Let us journey forward with faith, trusting in the promises of Christ, and rejoicing in the eternal reward that awaits us.

Lenten Reflection: What are the crosses you are currently

trying to carry? Do you try to manage that task on your own? Take a moment to ask Jesus to slip in beside you to help you carry your cross.

Day 3
Friday after Ash Wednesday

March 7, 2025

Isaiah 58:1–9a

Psalm 51:3–4, 5–6ab, 18–19

Matthew 9:14–15

"This, rather, is the fasting that I wish: releasing those bound unjustly, untying the thongs of the yoke; Setting free the oppressed, breaking every yoke;

Sharing your bread with the hungry, sheltering the oppressed and the homeless; Clothing the naked when you see them, and not turning your back on your own."

(Isaiah 58:6–7)

Fasting is a theme woven through both Isaiah and Matthew today. For the Jewish people, expressing gratitude to God for His abundant gifts was of paramount importance. They did this by returning a portion of those gifts to the Giver, an act of devotion that dates back to the earliest days of their faith, seen in the burnt offerings of Abraham. The central act of worship in the Jerusalem Temple was not only the sacrifice of a lamb but the offering of all kinds of food, symbolizing their dependence on God. Yet, beyond

9

these public acts of worship, there was a more private, intimate form of devotion: fasting. By abstaining from food, the faithful were reminded of their utter reliance on God's favor. Fasting is more than just a physical act; it is a spiritual discipline that sharpens our awareness of our deep need for God. As the saying goes, "Always give without remembering and always receive without forgetting."[i]

In Isaiah, God reveals that what would please Him even more than offerings in the Temple or fasting is to take that same food and reach out to those in need, offering it to them instead. We were created for communion—communion with our Creator and communion with one another. This sacred connection was broken in Eden, leading to a world where self-interest often overrides self-sacrifice. However, the sacrificial act of fasting, when extended beyond the altar to feed the hungry, begins to restore that original communion. It's a reminder that our faith is not just vertical, between us and God, but also horizontal, extending to those around us. Standing in solidarity with the hungry, the homeless, the imprisoned, and the burdened transforms a simple act of social justice into a profound act of sacrificial worship that glorifies God. Jesus emphasized this teaching, making it the central criterion by which we will be judged. For Christians, love is never merely an emotion; it is a behavior, a deliberate choice, a way of living that reflects God's own love for us.

"We make a living by what we get, but we make a life by what we give."[ii] During this holy season, while giving food, clothing, and shelter is vital, consider expanding your list of gifts. Give away your time by visiting the sick or calling someone who is homebound. Offer a smile to a stranger, a compliment, a gentle touch, a kind word, or a simple gesture that shows you care. It's often in these small, seemingly insignificant moments that we truly embody the love of Christ. These acts, though simple, can be transformative, both for those who receive them and for us as givers.

As we journey through this sacred season, let us remember that fasting, prayer, and almsgiving are not ends in themselves, but means by which we draw closer to God and each other. They are opportunities to live out the love we have received from Christ, to be His hands and feet in a world that desperately needs His light. Often, it is the smallest, most inexpensive acts that hold the greatest value, for they are given with a heart full of love and a spirit that reflects God's grace. Let us embrace this time as a chance to grow in love, deepen our faith, and be transformed by the simple yet profound act of giving from the heart. In doing so, we not only honor God but also bring hope, joy, and love to those around us, embodying the true spirit of Christ in our daily lives.

Lenten Reflection: Ask yourself how you can actually touch the life of the living person today by giving something of yourself away.

Day 4

Saturday after Ash Wednesday

March 6, 2025

Isaiah 58:9b–14

Psalm 86:1–2, 3–4, 5–6

Luke 5:27–32

"The Pharisees and their scribes complained to his disciples, saying, 'Why do you eat and drink with tax collectors and sinners?'"

(Luke 5:30)

God the Father deeply cares for the oppressed, the afflicted, and those who are powerless. Throughout His ministry, Jesus embraced and amplified the Jewish tradition of caring for the poor and disenfranchised, expanding the definition of neighbor to encompass all humanity. The parable of the Good Samaritan is a profound reminder that everyone—regardless of status, background, or belief—is our brother or sister. It challenges us to see beyond societal boundaries and recognize the inherent dignity in every person.

In the times when Scripture was written, society accepted slavery and often devalued individual human life. Large segments of the population endured unimaginable hardship, much as many still do today. Misery was rampant then, just as it is now. While people, including their rulers, often turn a blind eye to the suffering around them, Scripture makes it abundantly clear that God does not. This truth is powerfully revealed in the compassion, grief, sadness, kindness, and attentive care that Jesus extended to the most marginalized and outcast of His day.

Jesus's ministry was a living testament to God's unwavering commitment to those whom society deems unworthy. He didn't just preach love—He lived it. He sought out the lost, healed the sick, and restored dignity to those who had been cast aside. In every interaction, Jesus exemplified the heart of God, showing us that divine love is not reserved for a select few but is generously extended to all.

The final judgment scene described by Jesus in Matthew 25:35–46 underscores how critically important our treatment of others is to the Creator. Responding to human suffering is not merely an option for those who worship the God of Abraham; it is a divine mandate. The Trinitarian nature of God, as revealed by Christ, defines God in terms of communion and relationship. We are all created in the image and likeness of this triune God, and therefore, our communion with others is essential to becoming whole according to God's design.

The kingdom we pray for in the Our Father is not something that will simply descend from heaven; it is a reality that must be built, person by person, through our actions. As we lift up the poor among us, embrace the outcast, and extend love to all, we participate in bringing God's kingdom to earth. Every act of kindness, every moment of compassion, every effort to restore justice, brings us closer to the divine vision of a world united in love. This is the kingdom where every person is seen, valued, and cherished—where God's love is made manifest in our relationships and our communities.

As we strive to live out this calling, let us remember that we are not alone in this mission. The same Spirit that empowered Jesus empowers us. Each step we take in love, each hand we extend in service, builds up the kingdom of God in our midst. Let us move forward with hope and determination, knowing that our efforts, no matter how small, are part of God's grand design to heal and restore the world. Together, let us be the hands and feet of Christ, working to create a world where love, justice, and peace reign supreme. The kingdom of God is near—let us help bring it to life.

Lenten Reflection: Is there a group of people for whom I have little sympathy? Can you see them as your tax collector and welcome them to your table? What would Jesus do?

Day 5

First Sunday of Lent

Deuteronomy 26:1–11

Psalm 91:1–2, 9–16

Romans 10:8b–13

Luke 4:1–13

"You shall not put the Lord, your God, to the test."

(Luke 4:12)

Do you ever find your mind wandering in countless directions when you try to pray? It's a common struggle, yet it serves as a reminder to anchor your thoughts in the One who is steadfast: *"Trust in the Lord forever! For the Lord is an eternal rock"* (Isaiah 26:4).

In Deuteronomy 26, God provides a powerful example of how His people are to respond to His blessings. The annual harvest, a gift from God, was to be shared with the Levites—who had no inheritance of land—the widows, the orphans, and the foreigners among them. This practice was not merely a ritual; it was a divine invitation to recognize God's ongoing provision. Inspired by this command, the Jewish people extended their gratitude beyond a yearly tithe. They cultivated a habit of thankfulness, offering prayers of gratitude at every meal (Deuteronomy 8:10). The Talmud later built on this scriptural foundation, prescribing specific prayers before and after meals (Berakhot 48b).

To the nonbeliever, such practices might seem burdensome, as though they were just another set of rules to appease an unreachable deity. But to the believer, the truth is clear: God does not need our thanks; we need to give it. Gratitude transforms our hearts. It elevates our minds above the temporal and material, drawing us into the presence of the Divine. Prayer is not merely about uttering words; it is about communion with our Heavenly Father, who longs for a relationship with each of us.

Jesus exemplified this communion throughout His ministry. His life was a continuous prayer, a constant turning to the Father. Before performing miracles—whether multiplying loaves and fish to feed thousands, raising Lazarus from the dead, or healing the sick—Jesus gave thanks to the Father. Even in the simple act of eating, He offered prayers of gratitude. When faced with Satan's temptations in Gethsemane, the true battle was about where Jesus would place His focus. The enemy tempted Him to find satisfaction in the physical, to seek meaning and power in the world's offerings. "Look at your hunger, Jesus. Look at the kingdoms of the world, the power and glory within your reach. Look at your doubts and let them lead you away from God." Yet, Jesus looked only to the Father. His gaze never wavered. In the New Testament, Jesus is recorded as praying to the Father 38 times, and the words "thanks" or "thanksgiving" appear 72 times.

So, what is the message for us? It is simple yet profound: Keep your eyes on God. When Adam and Eve shifted their focus from the Creator to the serpent, they set in motion their downfall. But we are called to something higher: *"Rejoice always. Pray without ceasing. In all circumstances give thanks, for this is the will of God for you in Christ Jesus"* (1 Thessalonians 5:16-18). Prayer is not about following rules; it is about remaining in the presence of the One who gives life.

In a world full of distractions and challenges, it is easy to lose sight of what truly matters. Yet, we are invited to return to the simplicity and purity of a life centered on God. Stand in the light of God's love, and you will find yourself growing, flourishing in ways you never imagined. Let your prayers be rooted in gratitude, and let that gratitude guide your steps each day. As you keep your eyes fixed on God, you will discover a peace that transcends understanding and a joy that fills your heart, no matter the circumstances. The more you focus on Him, the more you will see His hand at work in your life, leading you toward a deeper, richer communion with the Creator who loves you beyond measure.

Lenten Reflection: How can you build into your life the

habit of turning to the Father in prayer throughout your day?

Day 6

Monday of First Week of Lent

March 10, 2025

Leviticus 19:1–2, 11–18

Psalm 19:8, 9, 10, 15

Matthew 25:31–46

"When the Son of Man comes in his glory, and all the angels with him, he will sit upon his glorious throne, and all the nations will be assembled before him. And he will separate them one from another, as a shepherd separates the sheep from the goats."

(Matthew 25:31–32)

For the first forty years of television, the Name of Jesus Christ was never uttered by characters on screen. Small businesses in inner cities faced challenges, but none were forced to close due to theft. The poorest immigrant districts of Harlem, Little Italy, and Chinatown in major cities were vibrant tourist destinations, celebrated for their specialty foods and cultural festivities. The police, clergy of all faiths, and the men and women of the military were held in high regard. The Pledge of Allegiance to the American flag marked the beginning of every public and private school day.

The culture described above was deeply rooted in the Judeo-Christian ethic. Our Scripture readings for Mass today, from Leviticus and Matthew, encapsulate the values of this ethic as it is meant to be lived out in the world. These values call us to hold God's name and the good name of our fellow citizens in reverence. They forbid theft and injustice, demanding respect for the work and property of others. They champion a civil society where discourse replaces violence, where hatred, grudges, revenge, and malicious speech are overcome by communication, love, and a concerted effort to recognize and appreciate the gifts each person brings to the table.

Today, we witness the near-collapse of traditional religious faith and the institutions that uphold it. The relentless propaganda machine works tirelessly to dig up every embarrassing moment of corruption by religious people over the past two thousand years, attempting to convince the masses that Jews, Christians, and religious individuals are inherently racist, materialistic, and exploitative of the powerless. In a world where media ownership often equates to control over truth, many adults in Western society have little to no understanding of the profound impact the Judeo-Christian tradition has had on shaping civil society. We are only beginning to grasp its value now, as we watch its influence being systematically erased from the social fabric.

The word "gospel" means "good news." The God of Israel, and those who believe in Him, have made our modern world possible by building communities shaped by the Word of God. This God has a plan and purpose for humanity, a plan that will continue to unfold despite the efforts of those who seek to silence the proclamation of this good news. The Judeo-Christian ethic that once shaped our society is not a relic of the past but a living, breathing force that has the power to transform hearts and rebuild communities.

As we reflect on the challenges of our times, let us remember that we are called to be bearers of this good news. We are called to live out the values of love, justice, and respect in our daily lives, standing as witnesses to the enduring power of God's Word. Even in the face of adversity, we can hold fast to the truth that God's kingdom will come, and His divine will shall be done on earth as it is in heaven.

Let us pray today with renewed hope and determination, trusting that God's light will shine through the darkness. May we be instruments of His peace, spreading the message of the gospel with courage and compassion. The world needs the good news now more than ever, and we are called to be its messengers. In faith, we can make a difference, one act of love at a time. God's plan is unfolding, and His grace is sufficient for every challenge we face. Let us go forth with confidence, knowing that the gospel is indeed the good news that will transform our world.

Lenten Reflection: Our Judeo-Christian tradition is a gift to the world from the hand of God.

Reread Leviticus 19:1–18 and list the good things that are only possible when God's rules are taken seriously.

Day 7

Tuesday of First Week of Lent

March 11, 2025

Isaiah 55:10–11

Psalm 34:4–7, 16–19

Matthew 6:7–15

*"Our Father in heaven, hallowed be your name, your
kingdom come, your will be done, on earth as in heaven.
Give us today our daily bread; and forgive us our debts, as we
forgive our debtors; and do not subject us to the final test, but
deliver us from the evil one."*

(Matthew 6:9b–13)

Isaiah reminds us today that God's Word is like rain
that falls from heaven, making the earth fertile and
fruitful. This same life-giving Word is spoken by Jesus
in our Gospel as He teaches us to pray the Our Father.
If we truly live out the words of this prayer, our lives
and the world around us will flourish and bloom in
God's grace.

This prayer is, first and foremost, a prayer of
community: "Our Father," "Give us," "Forgive us."
From the very beginning, it calls us to recognize that
we are not isolated individuals but part of a larger

24

family, a community of believers. The Creator intended for us to see one another as brothers and sisters, united in love and purpose. The ultimate goal of religious life is communion—communion with God and communion with one another. When we say, "Hallowed be Your name," we acknowledge that God is holy, sanctified, and transcendent—beyond our material world and the almighty Creator of all that exists. His Word should be the center of our lives, guiding every decision and action.

"Your kingdom come" is a powerful call for the restoration of the communion of love and peace that humanity once knew in the Garden of Eden. Christ commissions us to build that kingdom here on earth, so that we may one day enter its heavenly fulfillment. When we pray, "Your will be done," we open our hearts to the Holy Spirit, inviting divine guidance into our lives. The Spirit leads us to live in the way of Jesus, to be faithful disciples who listen, obey, and act with love.

"Give us today our daily bread" reminds us to live in the present moment, trusting that God provides for us each day. We are called to focus on the blessings God gives us today, rather than being consumed with worries about the future or regrets about the past. By trusting in God's provision, we step into a deeper relationship with Him, one that is rooted in faith and trust. Through this prayer, we also ask for the grace to "forgive," because love demands that we release our grievances and desires for revenge, carrying our cross and walking the Way of Jesus.

There is no true Christianity without the cross. Embracing the cross always involves letting go—surrendering our lives completely into God's hands. Forgiveness flows freely from Christ and is required of anyone who would follow Him. We pray, "Deliver us from evil," acknowledging that we can never afford to be self-satisfied or proud. Without a constant focus on God's blessings, we risk losing our humanity, slipping into a state where we are no more than creatures driven by base instincts.

As we reflect on the words of the Our Father, let us remember that this prayer is not just a set of words to be recited, but a powerful expression of our faith and trust in God. It is a call to live in communion with our Creator and with each other, to seek His kingdom, to do His will, and to trust in His provision. By embracing the teachings of this prayer, we allow God's grace to transform our hearts and our lives.

Let us go forward with renewed faith, knowing that God's Word will always bear fruit in our lives when we live according to His will. With each step we take in faith, we draw closer to the fulfillment of His promises, and we become a living testament to the power of His love. May we find strength in the words of this prayer, and may they guide us to live lives that reflect the light and love of Christ. In doing so, we become beacons of hope and instruments of God's peace in the world.

Lenten Reflection: Who have you had a difficult time forgiving? Letting go is only possible with the Spirit. Do you stay fixed in the present day and its blessings, or do you dwell in the past or future?

Day 8
Wednesday of First Week of Lent

March 12, 2025

Jonah 3:1–10

Psalm 51:3–4, 12–13, 18–19

Luke 11:29–32

"At the judgment the men of Nineveh will arise with this generation and condemn it, because at the preaching of Jonah they repented, and there something greater than Jonah here."

(Luke 11:32)

Jonah preached, and the people of Nineveh took him seriously. They examined their lives, reflected deeply on their actions, regretted how they had been living, and made a heartfelt and honest decision to change. What a powerful response! I can't help but feel a bit envious of Jonah. After forty-six years as a priest, I sometimes wonder if I've made much of a difference in people's lives. Many pastors across mainline Christian churches share this sentiment, watching with heavy hearts as their parishes close, their congregations dwindle, and the younger generation seems to drift away from religious education programs. It's easy to feel disillusioned, to wonder if the message of the Gospel is still reaching people in a world that seems increasingly indifferent.

And yet, despite these challenges, there is something—and Someone—far greater than Jonah here, right now, today. His name is Jesus. He is the Son of God, the very Word through whom you and I came into existence. He is the Good Shepherd who guides us, the Gate through which we enter, the Door that leads to eternal life. He is the Living Water that quenches our deepest thirst, the Lamb of God who takes away the sin of the world, the Alpha and the Omega, the Bread of Life, the Resurrection, and Life itself. Jesus is God in flesh and blood, who came to earth with a personal invitation for each of us to join Him in eternity. He has gone before us to prepare a place for us, and He is faithful to His promise, returning to take us one by one into His everlasting arms. This is the Good News—the most incredible news! And it is news we cannot keep to ourselves if we truly care about our brothers and sisters who wander this world so aimlessly, searching for meaning and purpose.

Consider those who have had near-death experiences and later report seeing a light after they "died." That light is Jesus. When our time comes, it is not an angel who will lead us to the other side but Jesus Himself. He will take us by the hand and guide us into

His Kingdom. The teachings of Jesus are a priceless gift that can bring meaning and fulfillment to lives that might otherwise feel empty. Living the Way of Jesus is the missing piece that can complete us as individuals, offering us a peace that no human being, no earthly power, and no material possession can ever provide.

There is something greater than Jonah here, and His name is Jesus. Believe in Him, embrace His teachings, and truly live! Let this truth fill your heart, transform your life, and inspire you to share the Good News with everyone you meet. For in Jesus, we find not only the answers to life's deepest questions but also the very source of life itself.

In moments of doubt or weariness, remember that Jesus walks with us, guiding our steps, and illuminating our path. He has not abandoned us, nor will He ever. His presence is the assurance that our efforts in His name are never in vain. As we continue to sow seeds of faith, love, and hope, trust that Jesus will bring forth the harvest, even when we cannot see it ourselves. The impact of His love is eternal, reaching far beyond what our eyes can perceive.

So, let us go forth with renewed courage and conviction, knowing that we are part of a divine story that God is still writing. Let us be bold in proclaiming the love of Christ, confident that He is at work in ways we may never fully understand. And let us find joy in the truth that Jesus is the Way, the Truth, and the Life, leading us and all whom we encounter into the fullness of life He promises. The journey is not easy, but with Jesus, it is a journey filled with hope, purpose, and the assurance of eternal life.

Lenten Reflection: Witnessing to Jesus does not always mean talking about religion or reminding people of the obligation to worship. Just be as faithful to Jesus as you can and live like he did to the best of your ability. Let go and let God!

Day 9

Thursday of First Week of Lent

March 13, 2025

Esther C:12, 14–16, 23–25

Psalm 138:1–3, 7–8

Matthew 7:7–12

"Queen Esther, seized with mortal anguish . . . afflicted her body severely. . . Then she prayed to the Lord, the God of Israel, saying: 'My Lord, our King, you alone are God. Help me, who am alone and have no help but you.' "

(Esther C:12a, 13b, 14)

If you have ever truly loved another human being, there will come a day when you find yourself, like Queen Esther, prostrate on the ground, pouring out your heart and begging God to hear your prayers. Esther faced the impending suffering of those she loved dearly. Though she was a queen, she had no real power to change the course of events. Despite her title, she didn't even own the clothes on her back; she lived at the mercy of a king who held all authority. But Esther possessed something far more powerful than earthly possessions or influence—she had unwavering faith in God. So she turned to the Lord in prayer, lifting up the people she loved and pleading for His blessing and protection.

Jesus, too, has witnessed the depths of human suffering firsthand. He walked among us, experiencing the raw pain and anguish that so often accompany our earthly journey. He knows what it is like to look into the tear-filled eyes of a mother burying her child, to sense the overwhelming guilt and shame that can make a person believe their life is a mistake, that they are worthless. Jesus has seen the blind begging for a glimpse of light, the crippled sitting hopeless, feeling as if they have no place or purpose in this world. He has felt the gnawing pangs of hunger and watched in sorrow as children wasted away for lack of bread. He has stood witness to the crushing injustice that falls so heavily on the poor and marginalized. Jesus wept with compassion, and even now, He invites us to bring our burdens to Him in prayer.

"Ask, and it will be given to you; seek, and you will find; knock, and the door will be opened to you" (Matthew 7:7). Though your suffering may not immediately cease when you pray, one thing is certain—you will never have to carry your cross alone. Jesus will come to you, and He will lift that heavy burden, sharing the weight of your pain and walking beside you every step of the way. He has promised never to leave you, never to forsake you, because, just like Esther, your name—and

the name of every person you love—is carved into the palm of His hand.

Even now, in His resurrected and glorified state, Jesus still bears the scars of His crucifixion as a testament to His love and sacrifice for you. He knows your heartache; He understands your struggles. He invites you to go to Him, to place your trust in Him, and to allow Him to carry not just your burdens, but your very soul. In those moments of deepest despair, when all you can do is cry out to God, remember that He is already there, waiting to embrace you with His unfailing love and grace.

So go to Him. He is waiting with open arms, ready to lift you up and carry you through whatever trials you face, just as He carried the cross for all of humanity. Let your heart find peace in His presence, knowing that you are never alone and that the God who loves you beyond measure will always be by your side. Whatever burden you bear, whatever sorrow you carry, place it in His hands and trust that He will guide you through. With Jesus, there is always hope, always a path forward, and always the promise of new life.

Lenten Reflection: What weighs on your heart today? Lift it up and surrender your prayer to the Lord.

Day 10

Friday of First Week of Lent

March 14, 2025

Ezekiel 18:21–2

Psalm 130:1–8

Matthew 5:20–26

"If you bring your gift to the altar, and there recall that your brother has anything against you, leave your gift there at the altar; go first and be reconciled with your brother, and then come and offer your gift."

(Matthew 5:23–24)

It can be surprising, and perhaps even disheartening, to witness the cynicism often directed toward prisoners who claim to have found Jesus. Society frequently shows little mercy for those who have committed crimes, and there is a deep-seated resentment when sentences are reduced. Many believe that justice is not fully served unless an individual completes their entire sentence behind bars. This skepticism extends to the notion that someone with a history of wrongdoing could genuinely experience a profound change of heart. The immediate assumption is that any claimed conversion is a mere manipulation—a strategic move to deceive the parole board and secure an early release.

Yet, the first Scripture reading today from Ezekiel challenges this cynical view, suggesting that God Himself believes in the possibility of jailhouse conversions. The passage reminds us that even those who have walked the path of wickedness can turn their lives around, committing themselves to doing what is "right and just." It is a powerful reminder that transformation is not only possible but is something God deeply desires for all His children. The teachings of Jesus further affirm this belief in the power of conversion. Christ's words in Matthew 5:24, *"Leave your gift there at the altar . . . and be reconciled with your brother,"* call us to a life of reconciliation, forgiveness, and peace. Jesus assumes that if we are truly worshipping at the altar, we believe in the power of transformation—not only for ourselves but for others as well.

However, the responsibility for right behavior extends beyond the individual Christian. While we are called to seek reconciliation, we must also recognize that we cannot control the actions or responses of others. We are only responsible for our own behavior and attitudes. Christ believes in our capacity to pursue peace and forgiveness, even when faced with difficult people and challenging circumstances. The focus of these Scripture passages is not solely on those who are incarcerated or have committed crimes; they are directed at each of us. They challenge us to reflect on our own attitudes, our own willingness to forgive, and our own belief in the power of redemption.

Jesus died for us, offering forgiveness for our sins, and now He expects us to live in a way that reflects that grace. We are called to decide—every day—to forgive, to extend the same mercy that has been given to us. And when we approach others, whether they are in prison or not, we must do so with the belief that they too can be touched by the Holy Spirit and genuinely desire reconciliation. We must drop the cynicism that so easily creeps into our hearts. It is unbecoming of a Christian and stands in stark contrast to the message of the Gospel.

God's grace is boundless, His love is transformative, and His belief in our ability to change is unwavering. If God can believe in the possibility of a sinner's conversion, so should we. We are called to be instruments of His peace, bearers of His forgiveness, and living testimonies of the power of His love. So, let go of the cynicism, embrace the hope that Christ offers, and believe in the possibility of transformation—not just for others, but for ourselves as well.

As we move forward, let us open our hearts to the boundless possibilities that God's grace offers. Trust in the power of forgiveness and the transformative love that Christ exemplifies. Each day, we have the opportunity to be a beacon of hope and compassion in a world that so desperately needs it. With faith and a willingness to see the good in others, we can make a difference. Remember, no one is beyond the reach of God's love, and every soul is capable of redemption. In believing this, we not only honor God's faith in us, but we also become a source of His light to those who are lost and searching for a way back home.

Lenten Reflection: Is there someone living or deceased you need to forgive before you leave your gift at the altar? The Holy Spirit was sent to help you do this. Ask for help. Let go!

Day 11

Saturday of First Week of Lent

March 15, 2025

Deuteronomy 26:16–19

Psalm 119:1–2, 4–5, 7–8

Matthew 5:43–48

[Jesus said:] "But I say to you, love your enemies, and pray for those who persecute you, that you may be children of your heavenly Father."

(Matthew 5:44–45)

There is no way you can avoid feeling pain if someone sticks a knife in your belly! God designed us with the capacity to feel pain for a reason—it serves as a crucial alert system, warning us of serious injury or harm. This is true not only physically but emotionally as well. When Jesus commands us to "love your enemies," He isn't suggesting that we should feel good or comfortable around those who wish us harm. In fact, there are times when it might be wise to avoid such individuals altogether, depending on the situation. Our natural feelings when confronted with an enemy—whether it's anxiety, fear, anger, resentment, or bitterness—are a direct result of our human wiring. It's perfectly normal to have these emotions when faced with someone who has hurt us or poses a threat. Consider the difference between someone speaking unkindly about you and someone actively trying to get you fired from your job. The intensity of your feelings would understandably vary in these situations. All emotions exist on a spectrum, ranging from mild discomfort to intense distress. But here's the key: when Jesus asks us to love our enemies, He is not giving us instructions on how to feel. Instead, He is teaching us how to act.

The love that Jesus speaks of in this context is not about emotions—it's about behavior. We may not have much control over our initial feelings, but we do have significant power over our actions. Despite the negative emotions we might feel, we can choose how we respond to our enemies. We can decide to search for and acknowledge the good qualities in someone who opposes us. We can refuse to engage in gossip, even if the stories we could share are true and damaging to their reputation. We can choose to speak words of kindness, warmth, and engagement, even to those who have wronged us. A simple smile in the presence of an enemy can be a powerful act of defiance against the cycle of negativity. We can consciously decide not to bring up past hurts or the wrongs that an enemy has done, choosing instead to let go of our desire for revenge or even what we perceive as justice. In doing so, we embrace mercy—the same mercy that Jesus has shown to each of us.

This is the heart of Christian love: the choice to act in a way that reflects the character of Jesus, even when it's hard, even when it goes against our natural inclinations. No one ever said that following Christ would be easy! Loving our enemies is one of the most challenging commands in the Gospel. It calls us to rise above our base instincts, to transcend our immediate feelings, and to live out a love that is active and intentional. It's about doing what is right, not what is easy.

So, when you find yourself confronted with an enemy, remember that Jesus isn't asking you to change how you feel—He's asking you to change how you act. Choose mercy over judgment, kindness over retaliation, and love over hate. It may not be easy, but it is the path that leads to true peace and the fulfillment of our calling as followers of Christ. Christianity isn't about taking the easy road; it's about walking the path that is right, a path that mirrors the love and grace of our Savior.

As you navigate the complexities of human relationships, keep in mind that the way we treat others, especially those who challenge us, is a reflection of the love Christ has shown to us. By choosing to act in love, even when it feels impossible, we not only grow closer to God but also become vessels of His peace in a troubled world. Every act of kindness, every decision to forgive, every moment of mercy plants seeds of transformation—both in our hearts and in the hearts of those around us. And in the end, this journey of love, difficult as it may be, is the one that leads us to a deeper understanding of God's infinite grace and the true joy of living in His light.

Lenten Reflection: Is there anyone against whom you hold a grudge? Do you need reconciliation with someone? What are you going to do about it?

Day 12

Second Sunday of Lent

March 16, 2025

Genesis 15:1–12, 17–18

Psalm 33

Philippians 3:17–4:1

Luke 9:28–36

THE TRANSFIGURATION OF JESUS

"At that time some Pharisees came to him and said, 'Go away, leave this area because Herod wants to kill you.'"

(Luke 13:31)

If I asked you to list what you need to survive, starting with the most important item, you'd probably begin with food and water, maybe shelter. If you thought about it more, you might add sleep—because people do need sleep to survive. But if this is your list, you've forgotten the most essential need of all. What do people need even more than food, water, shelter, and sleep to survive? People need to feel safe. Safety is the most fundamental need for human survival. If you were fleeing an enemy, you would forgo food, water, shelter, and sleep, and keep running until you dropped. Safety is the priority above all else.

This critical need for safety is often exploited during elections to influence voters. Just create an enemy and convince people they are in danger. Even if the new leaders tell you they will raise taxes and curb your rights, most people are willing to pay any price to feel secure. The candidate who makes people feel safe is the one who gets elected.

In our first reading from Genesis, we see Abraham feeling anything but safe. He has no male heir, and this means his name will die out with him. In a time when people did not believe in life after death, not passing on your name was akin to eternal death—complete annihilation. Abraham is terrified that this will be his fate. God, understanding his fear, reassures him by promising descendants as numerous as the stars in the sky.

In the Gospel, the Pharisees approach Jesus and warn Him that He is not safe—they've heard that Herod wants Him dead. How does Jesus respond to this threat? He acknowledges the danger. He knows Herod is a fox who will likely follow through with his plans. Jesus even knows where His life will end—in Jerusalem. Yet, what is striking is that Jesus refuses to live in fear. He tells His listeners that He will continue with His mission—healing, casting out demons, and preaching the Gospel. He chooses not to be governed by the need for safety because He has taken a leap of faith, trusting completely in the Father.

Remember the prayer Jesus taught us, the Our Father? "Give us this day our daily bread." Jesus isn't just talking about physical bread here. He's encouraging us to make a choice to stay in the present, to trust that no matter what happens, the Father is with us and will provide for our needs. While we can't stop bad things from happening in this world, we can choose not to let them rule our lives. We can choose to let God rule our lives.

Give God your heart, your mind, your strength, and your spirit, and let Him be the one to worry about your safety. God is all you really need to live your life in peace, not an MK47. Place your trust in Him, and you will find that the peace He offers surpasses all understanding. In a world filled with uncertainties and fears, let the assurance of God's presence be your fortress, guiding you through every trial with the promise of His unwavering love and protection. Trust in God, for in Him, you will always be safe.

Lenten Reflection: Can you remember a time when you didn't feel safe? Disease? Work or people? Something on the news? Did you ever bring your faith in Jesus into the moment when you were afraid? Can you bring Jesus into the moment now?

Day 13

Monday of Second Week of Lent

March 17, 2025

Daniel 9:4b–10

Psalm 79:8–9, 11, 13

Luke 6:36–38

[Jesus said to his disciples:] "Be merciful, just as (also) your Father is merciful."

(Luke 6:36)

To truly understand mercy, you first need a solid grasp of justice. Justice is about giving someone what they are rightfully due. For example, if you agree to buy my house for a certain amount, you can't show up at the closing with less and expect me to be satisfied. You promised a specific amount, so justice demands that you pay exactly what was agreed upon. That's what is due. Similarly, if you drink and drive, and the fine for a first offense is $400, justice requires that you pay the full fine—every cent.

Mercy, however, is not about giving someone what they deserve but rather about not giving them what they deserve. Mercy involves feeling compassion for the person who owes something, leading you to act differently. Perhaps someone agreed to pay a certain amount for a house, but then the husband is tragically killed while serving in the military, and now the widow can't meet the mortgage payments. Mercy steps in, feels compassion, and forgives the debt. It pushes justice aside and wipes the slate clean. Or consider someone caught drinking and driving, who owes a $400 fine. The judge, upon learning that the driver just discovered his daughter has terminal cancer, recognizes that justice demands the fine be paid, but instead, mercy intervenes. The judge, moved by compassion and convinced the offense won't be repeated, dismisses the fine and issues a warning.

A similar scenario plays out when a waitress provides poor service. Justice would demand she receive no tip and be reported to her manager, but mercy considers that she might be struggling with personal issues. Instead of reporting her, mercy leaves a tip and says nothing. Mercy is what happens when compassion is added to an interaction.

Many people express outrage when a criminal is released from prison early, believing that justice demands they serve the full sentence. Yet, parole hearings and judges exist because humanity has learned that sometimes maintaining our compassion as a society means taking the risk of extending mercy. Indeed, mercy is a gamble. The recipient might be manipulating you, or they might go back to their old ways. But mercy isn't always about the person who owes the debt; it's about the person to whom the debt is owed.

In our walk with Christ, we are called to consider how we imitate God's dealings with humanity. Our God is merciful, and as His children, we are called to reflect that divine mercy in our own lives. The prophet Micah reminds us, *"You have been told, O man, what is good, and what the Lord requires of you: Only to do the right and to love goodness, and to walk humbly with your God"* (Micah 6:8). To love goodness is to embrace mercy, to choose compassion over strict justice.

Jesus instructed His disciples, *"Be merciful, just as your Father is merciful"* (Luke 6:36). This command is not merely a suggestion; it is a call to embody the very nature of God in our daily interactions. Mercy allows us to experience and share the boundless love of God, a love that forgives, heals, and restores.

As you navigate your journey of faith, remember that showing mercy is not a sign of weakness but of profound strength. It is an opportunity to mirror the heart of God, to extend grace where it is undeserved, and to bring light into the darkest corners of the human experience. By choosing mercy, we participate in the divine work of transforming the world, one act of compassion at a time. So let us strive to be merciful, trusting that in doing so, we draw closer to the heart of

God and help to build a world that reflects His love and grace.

Lenten Reflection: Think of an instance when you were offended, cheated or talked about unfairly. How could you have responded with mercy?

Day 14
Tuesday of Second Week of Lent

March 18, 2025

Isaiah 1:10, 16–20

Psalm 50:8–9, 16–17, 21, 23

Matthew 23:1–12

"The greatest among you must be your servant. Whoever exalts himself will be humbled; but whoever humbles himself will be exalted."

(Matthew 23:11–12)

Isaiah doesn't hold back when he calls his listeners "princes of Sodom" and "people of Gomorrah." These cities had long been destroyed for their offenses against God, particularly for their inhospitality towards visiting angels. Isaiah's words are a sharp insult, designed to shock his audience into self-reflection. Yet, after delivering this harsh rebuke, Isaiah offers something absolutely wonderful, hopeful, and encouraging. He says, *"Come now, let us set things right"* (Isaiah 1:18). With these words, Isaiah suggests that everything can change in an instant with an act of will.

Similarly, Jesus is often stern with the Pharisees, condemning their inner corruption and their indifference to the burdens they place on the poor. But then, like Isaiah, Jesus extends an invitation: a call to act differently. He invites them—and us—to be humble, sensitive, kind, empathetic, and loving. With a single act of will, a choice, everything can change for the Pharisees and for anyone willing to accept this invitation.

As people who consider ourselves religious, we are following Scripture meditations during Lent, seeking to imitate Christ, walk in the Master's steps, and grow in the Holy Spirit. Yet, we know that talk is cheap. It's easy to feel good about ourselves as we give up chocolate or struggle to lose a few pounds during Lent. But deep down, we understand that faith is much more than words or giving up sweets. The ultimate test of faith is not in how much we tithe or how many rosaries we say, but in how we treat those who are without a voice, without money, without power.

In the Gospel of Matthew, Jesus reminds us, *"Whatever you did for one of these least brothers of mine, you did for me"* (Matthew 25:40). This is the heart of true faith— seeing Christ in the faces of the marginalized and acting with compassion and love.

Do you ever consider that, under different circumstances, it could be you walking two thousand miles to cross the southern border? Do you ever imagine what it might be like to spend your life savings to secure a dangerous journey from China to Ecuador, hoping to reach America? Have you wondered what it's like to grow up in an inner city where school is a daily battle of fights and chaos? Or to be raised in public housing with an absent or incarcerated parent? Jesus calls each of us to explore how we might become the servants of the servants, the lowest in the social order, and to act with the compassion and love that He so freely gives.

Let us remember that our faith is not just a personal journey but a communal one, where we are called to lift each other up, especially those who are most in need. Every small act of kindness, every gesture of love, has the power to change lives, including our own. So as we move forward in our faith, let us embrace the call to love more deeply, serve more humbly, and reflect the light of Christ in all we do. In doing so, we fulfill the commandment to love our neighbors as ourselves and bring the Kingdom of God a little closer to earth.

Lenten Reflection: Who is the one person I do not want to be humble before? How do I change that?

Day 15

Wednesday of Second Week of Lent

March 19, 2025

Jeremiah 18:18–20

Psalm 31:5–6, 14–16

Matthew 20:17–28

"Whoever wishes to be great among you shall be your servant; whoever wishes to be first among you shall be your slave. Just so, the Son of Man did not come to be served but to serve and to give his life as a ransom for many."

(Matthew 20:26–28)

Truly good people are often the targets of scorn. Even someone as revered as Mother Teresa has faced harsh criticism. Her Wikipedia article contains some pretty ugly accusations, including criticism of her work in the hospices she established for not providing medical care and claims of hypocritical deathbed baptisms. There are even links drawn to colonialism and racism. Reading it, you might think that the Missionaries of Charity sisters were shallow, heartless, and godless women, doing their work in Christ's name without any true compassion. And yet, these criticisms are taken seriously and believed by many. A large portion of the population sees only corruption in anyone associated with the Catholic Church.

Jesus warned us that those who choose to follow Him must expect the world's hatred. He wasn't exaggerating when He said, *"If the world hates you, realize that it hated me first"* (John 15:18). But what is truly disheartening is when the criticism comes not from outside the Church but from within. Bishop Fulton Sheen once spoke of the suspicion and ill will he faced from other clerics. Ask your choir director, your pastor, or the director of religious education in your parish if they receive encouragement and support from congregants. Or ask the dedicated teachers in your public schools how it is working with parents today. Those who genuinely strive to serve others must often expect a kind of crucifixion.

Consider the story of one pastor who, when told by a woman that her son was entering the seminary, broke down in heavy sobs. It took him a long time to compose himself, and when he did, he encouraged her to dissuade her son from becoming a priest. This reaction might seem extreme, but it reflects the reality of how we sometimes treat good people within our church and society. Crucifixion is a harsh word, but it's not far from the truth.

This may not be what you want to hear about serving others in today's world, but it's the reality. The way of Lent is a journey to the cross. Jesus walked step by painful step over the countryside, His sandals worn and His feet bleeding. Yet He kept going, one step at a time. Why did He do it? Why do you continue to serve, despite the challenges? The answer is simple: love.

Love is the driving force behind every act of true service. It's what keeps us going when the world criticizes, mocks, or even betrays us. Jesus showed us that love is stronger than hate, stronger than fear, and stronger than any obstacle we might face. *"There is no fear in love, but perfect love drives out fear"* (1 John 4:18).

So, when the journey feels heavy, and the world's criticism weighs on your heart, remember that you are walking in the footsteps of Christ. You are participating in His love, His sacrifice, and His ultimate victory. Keep going, one step at a time, knowing that your labor in the Lord is not in vain. In the end, love will triumph, and you will find yourself sharing in the resurrection joy that comes after the cross.

Lenten Reflection: How can I lift the burden a good person is carrying and encourage them to take one more step?

Day 16

Thursday of Second Week of Lent

Jeremiah 17:5–10

Psalm 1:1–5

Luke 16:19–31

"Thus says the LORD: *Cursed is the man who trusts in human beings, who seeks his strength in flesh, whose heart turns away from the* LORD.*"*

(Jeremiah 17:5)

How do you live in this world with your heart fixed on God? Jeremiah saw this as a serious issue in his time, observing that people seemed to trust in themselves, their own resources, public figures, or their wealth and status. God often seemed like an afterthought. Jesus also recognized this problem and shared many parables to encourage us to keep our hearts focused on the Father.

One powerful example is the parable of the rich man who ignored poor Lazarus at his gate and ultimately ended up in hell. This man lived comfortably without any thought of God. The only problem was that his time on earth had a finish line. This world is not our true home; it is merely a place of formation and testing. Our real home is with the Father.

In today's world, life can be so comfortable that it's easy for many abundantly blessed individuals to forget about the afterlife. It's enjoyable to go out for pizza on a Friday night or attend a baseball game. After a long day of work, it's tempting to escape into a great movie on Netflix or Prime. The reality of war and poverty can feel distant when you're driving to the mall or spending a day with your kids at the zoo. Modern life is filled with activities—endless sporting events, hobbies, and busy schedules—that keep us occupied and leave little time to seriously think about God. In fact, it's quite easy to live without thinking about God at all.

But then we are reminded of Jesus's parable about the rich man. The clock is ticking. This world is not our true home. You will only be complete as a human being when you are in communion with your Creator. He made you for His pleasure, not your own. So, take a moment to look around at your wonderful world and ask yourself who gave you these blessings, because they are indeed gifts. *"Every good giving and every perfect gift is from above, coming down from the Father of lights"* (James 1:17). You need to say something to the Giver of these gifts. You need to do something too—something for the Giver. Listening to His voice might be a good place to start. Centering your mind, heart, and spirit on loving the Giver should also be a priority in response to His abundant blessings. Just don't ignore God.

Don't be lukewarm. Indifference and apathy anger God. *"I, the Lord, am your God. . . You shall not have other gods besides me"* (Exodus 20:2-3).

In the end, the things of this world will fade away, but your relationship with God will last forever. Let your heart be fixed on Him, and in doing so, you will find true peace, purpose, and joy that transcends the temporary pleasures of this life. Embrace the blessings He has given you, and let your life be a reflection of His love and grace. Remember, your true home is with the Father, and He is waiting to welcome you with open arms.

Lenten Reflection: Is God the center of my life? Are all my thoughts and actions somehow connected to God's place in my heart? Swimming in this ocean of God's gifts, how do I keep my heart fixed on loving God?

Day 17

Friday of Second Week of Lent

March 21, 2025

Genesis 37:3–4, 12–13, 17–28

Psalm 105:18–21

Matthew 21:33–43, 45–46

"Did you never read in the scriptures: 'The stone that the builders rejected has become the cornerstone; by the Lord has this been done, and it wonderful in our eyes'?"

(Matthew 21:42)

The first reading from Genesis recounts the powerful story of Joseph, who was rejected by his brothers yet later became the very person who saved their lives during a devastating famine. In the Gospel of Matthew, the focus shifts to the ultimate rejection—Jesus, who was spurned by His own people, yet went on to save humankind from eternal damnation. Both Joseph and Jesus were like stones rejected by the builders, but in both cases, God the Father used the evil intended against them to bring about something profoundly good. As Psalm 118:22 says, *"The stone the builders rejected has become the cornerstone."*

Joseph endured unimaginable suffering: rejected by his own flesh and blood, cast into a pit where he faced hunger and despair, sold into slavery, and unjustly imprisoned. Jesus, too, faced the deepest depths of human suffering—rejection, ridicule, abandonment, torture, and crucifixion. All human suffering is inherently evil and irrational. Evil never makes sense to the rational mind because it is contrary to God's design. While God does not will evil, He does permit it and can even use our experiences of suffering within His divine plan to bring about a greater good.

Evil will inevitably intrude upon your life. It may manifest physically, mentally, relationally, or spiritually. It could come in the form of cancer, a car accident, a rupture in your marriage, addiction, depression, a natural disaster, war, the loss of a job, or betrayal by a close friend. Evil has many faces, and none of us are immune to its reach. If Christ Himself could not escape evil, neither can we. The critical question is not whether evil will try to destroy our peace—because it surely will—but rather, will we allow it to succeed? Will we let it dictate the course of our lives?

For both Joseph and Jesus, it was their close relationship with the Father that defined their responses to the harshest of circumstances. When faced with trials, they turned to the Father, making Him their rock and their refuge. It was their submission to the Father's will that ultimately stripped evil of its power, transforming their suffering into something redemptive and life-giving. In their stories, we see that while evil may have its moment, it does not have the final word. That final word belongs to God, and it is one of love, redemption, and hope. As Romans 8:28 reminds us, *"We know that all things work for good for those who love God, who are called according to his purpose."*

As we face our own trials, we are invited to follow the example of Joseph and Jesus, to cling to the Father, and to trust that He can bring good out of even the darkest situations. Let us remember that our suffering, when surrendered to God, can be transformed into something that not only strengthens us but also blesses others. Evil may try to shake our peace, but with God as our foundation, it can never take it away. With God, there is always hope, and in His hands, even our greatest trials can be turned into triumphs.

Lenten Reflection: Recall instances in your own life when evil (suffering) could have destroyed you. How did your faith in Jesus help you not just to survive but to be victorious? How did God work to bring good from evil in your life?

Day 18

Saturday of Second Week of Lent

Micah 7:14–15, 18–20

Psalm 103:1–4, 9–12

Luke 15:1–3, 11–32

"My son, you are here with me always; everything I have is yours. But now we must celebrate and rejoice, because your brother was dead and has come to life again; he was lost and has been found."

(Luke 15:31–32)

This Gospel story is often referred to as the story of the prodigal son, but the true focus is not on the son; it is on the father. The wayward son, who acts like a narcissistic, spoiled, and selfish young man, is not a unique character. There are countless individuals like him in our society today, even within our own families. However, the heart of this story lies in the father's boundless love, mercy, and compassion. Any parent reading this can easily identify with the father's plight and his profound love.

No matter how much our children falter, no matter how deeply they wound us or stray from the path we've hoped for them, there isn't a parent among us who wouldn't instantly embrace them if they were to "come to their senses." We long for the day when they recognize the beauty of faith in Jesus, the richness of a life lived in God's presence. Our prayers rise fervently, asking that they find love that is faithful and enduring, meaningful work, and a life of purpose. While we may not be concerned with what specific job they pursue, we know that true happiness is elusive without God. It cannot be found without a moral compass, without a deep understanding of right and wrong, without the willingness to sacrifice for something greater than oneself.

As parents, we are created in the image and likeness of God, and it is this divine reflection that guides our actions. Just as God's mercy triumphs over justice, so does our love for our children surpass any desire for strictness or punishment. We never want to be the stern parent who must draw hard boundaries or enforce rules, yet sometimes this role is necessary as we continue to pray, hope, and wait for our children to return to the values we've instilled in them. The psalmist reminds us, *"Merciful and gracious is the Lord, slow to anger, abounding in kindness"* (Psalm 103:8 NAB). This verse beautifully encapsulates the essence of God's love—a love that we, as parents, are called to emulate.

In the end, love, forgiveness, and compassion will always have the final say, both with God and with us. Our greatest hope is that, like the father in the parable, we will be there with open arms when our children find their way back to the path of faith, love, and righteousness. We are called to embody the same grace that God extends to each of us, trusting that no matter how far they stray, they are never beyond the reach of His love—or ours. The story of the prodigal son reminds us that in the face of mistakes and missteps, redemption is always possible, and it is this hope that sustains us as we journey alongside our children, believing in their potential for growth, transformation, and a return to the heart of God.

As we reflect on this parable, let us be encouraged that God's love is ever-present, and His mercy is without end. No matter where our loved ones are on their journey, we can trust that God's grace is at work, drawing them closer to Him, and that we, too, are held in that same, unfailing love.

Lenten Reflection: Imagine that you are the father in our story. Who is it in your own experience that you have shown mercy toward? Every one of us will repeatedly find ourselves in situations where we can make divine mercy present.

Day 19

Third Sunday of Lent

March 23, 2025

Exodus 3:1–8, 13–15

Psalm 103:1–8, 11   1

Corinthians 10:1–6, 10–12

Luke 13:1–9

" 'But,' said Moses to God, 'when I go to the Israelites and say to them, "The God of your fathers has sent me to you," if they ask me, "What is his name?" what am I to tell them?' God replied, 'I am who I am.' Then he added, 'This is what you shall tell the Israelites: I AM sent me to you.' "

(Exodus 3:13–14)

In ancient Middle Eastern cultures, it was widely believed that knowing the name of a god granted a person the power to summon that deity, thereby giving them a certain degree of influence over the divine. With a name came the perceived ability to make demands and request favors. However, when Moses asked the God of Israel for His name, God refused to be confined by human expectations. The response, "I AM WHO I AM," was not a name in the traditional sense, but a profound declaration of eternal existence. "I AM" signifies an ever-present, unchanging God—eternal, without beginning or end, immortal, and uncreated. The God of Israel, the one true God, allows no other gods to stand before Him. No creature, no human, can ever hope to exert control or wield power over the Creator, who reigns sovereign over all.

Fast forward to our Gospel reading for today's Mass, and we encounter the Pharisees questioning Jesus about this great "I AM." Recently, there had been tragic events—Pilate's brutal execution of a group of Galileans and the collapse of a tower that claimed eighteen lives. The Pharisees, true to their nature, speculated whether these deaths were divine punishment for hidden sins. But Jesus, in His wisdom, turned their question on its head. He suggested that the God of Israel does not need to engineer accidents or ruthless murders to convey His messages. The timing of death is unpredictable for everyone, and these recent tragedies are not indicators of divine wrath. Instead, Jesus calls upon the crowd to focus on their own spiritual vigilance, urging them to be mindful of their immortal souls: *"But I tell you, if you do not repent, you will all perish as they did!"* (Luke 13:5). Death can come in the blink of an eye, and thus, every person must live in readiness, faithfully adhering to God's commandments.

God expects each fig tree in His garden to bear fruit—fruit that nourishes and sustains. He will seek evidence of this fruitfulness when we stand before

Him, not in the form of wealth or status, but in acts of mercy, justice, and compassion. Feeding the hungry, working for justice, caring for the sick—these are the fruits that God desires from those who seek to enter His Kingdom. As it is written in Micah 6:8, "You have been told, O man, what is good, and what the Lord requires of you: Only to do justice and to love goodness, and to walk humbly with your God."

The God of Israel is indeed a serious farmer, one who expects a harvest from His crops. We are all called to examine the criteria Christ set forth for entry into His Kingdom. The end will come when we least expect it, and when it does, God will look for the fruits of our labor. Let us live each day with purpose, knowing that our actions have eternal significance, and strive to cultivate the love, compassion, and justice that reflect the heart of God.

In a world that often feels unpredictable and harsh, let us find comfort in the unchanging nature of God's love. His mercy is always available, and His call to us is clear: bear fruit, live justly, love with a full heart, and walk humbly with Him. With this commitment, we can stand confidently before our Creator, knowing we have lived lives that honor His eternal "I AM."

Lenten Reflection: If you are the fig tree in today's parable, can you name the specific fruit that God might be expecting from your life? What fruit might you offer Jesus today?

Day 20
Monday of Third Week of Lent

March 24, 2025

2 Kings 5:1–5

Psalm 42:2, 3; 43:3–4

Luke 4:24–30

[Jesus said,] " 'There were many lepers in Israel during the time of Elisha the prophet; yet not one of them was cleansed, but only Naaman the Syrian.' When the people in the synagogue heard this, they were all filled with fury."

(Luke 4:27–28)

The season of Lent is a time when many Catholics seek out opportunities to celebrate the Sacrament of Reconciliation, or as it was traditionally known, "go to Confession." Perhaps you've encountered someone who says they don't believe in Confession, arguing that they can confess their sins directly to God, believing it's the same as participating in the sacrament. To them, sitting in front of a priest seems unnecessary. After all, if God desires to forgive, He can do so wherever we are—no priest required.

In a sense, these individuals are correct. The Catholic Church teaches that true contrition and a sincere request for God's forgiveness indeed "removes the sin." It is true that you can confess your sins in private, and God, in His infinite mercy, hears and forgives. *"If we acknowledge our sins, he is faithful and just and will forgive our sins and cleanse us from every wrongdoing"* (1 John 1:9). This scripture affirms the power of personal repentance and God's willingness to forgive.

But what about the sacrament of Confession? Does it still hold significance in our faith? To explore this, we can learn from the story of Naaman in 2 Kings 5:1–5. Naaman, an army commander of the king of Aram and a pagan, suffered from leprosy. When a slave girl mentioned that a prophet in Israel could cure his disease, Naaman set out on a journey to find this prophet. Eventually, he encountered Elisha, who provided him with seemingly simple instructions: *"Go and wash seven times in the Jordan"* (5:10) Naaman's initial reaction mirrored the skepticism some feel about Confession today. He was enraged. Why should he wash in the muddy waters of the Jordan when cleaner, more impressive rivers existed back home? It didn't make sense to him. Why couldn't the God of Israel heal him on the spot with a simple command? And why wash seven times—why not just once? The whole idea seemed absurd to Naaman, and he decided to return home without following through.

However, as Naaman turned away in anger, his servants reasoned with him, persuading him to at least try, since he had nothing to lose. Reluctantly, Naaman obeyed, washing seven times as instructed—and he was miraculously healed. This story teaches us a profound truth: God chooses how He will act. He doesn't always align with our expectations or logic. God chose to pass on the power of the keys to bind and loose sin to the apostles, a power that has been exercised through the sacrament of Reconciliation for two thousand years. As Jesus said to His disciples, "Whose sins you forgive are forgiven them, and whose sins you retain are retained" (John 20:23). This passage highlights the unique role of the Church in administering God's forgiveness through the sacraments.

God's ways are often mysterious, but they are purposeful. Any priest who has spent years hearing confessions can attest to the profound healing that occurs when sins, carried like heavy burdens for years, are finally surrendered to God and released. The Sacrament of Reconciliation is more than just a ritual; it's a divine encounter where God's mercy meets our humanity, bringing us back into the embrace of His love. As we reflect on Naaman's story, we're reminded that God's instructions, though sometimes difficult to understand, are always rooted in His desire for our healing and wholeness.

So, let us approach the Sacrament of Reconciliation with open hearts, trusting that in His infinite wisdom, God knows what is best for us. Let us find peace in His mercy, knowing that no sin is too great to be forgiven, no burden too heavy to be lifted. And as we leave the confessional, may we carry with us the assurance that we are deeply loved, fully forgiven, and called to live in the light of His grace.

Lenten Reflection: Think about the Sacrament of Reconciliation. Why do you think God gave us this Sacrament when individuals can receive forgiveness privately simply by asking?

Day 21

The Annunciation of the Lord

March 25, 2025

Isaiah 7:10–14; 8:10

Hebrews 10:4–10

Luke 1:26–38

"Therefore the Lord himself will give you this sign: the virgin shall be with child, and bear a son, and shall name him Immanuel," which means "With us is God!"

(Isaiah 7:14; 8:10)

March 25 falls exactly nine months before December 25, marking the celebration of the Solemnity of the Annunciation during Lent. On this day, we reflect on the moment when history was forever changed by a young woman's profound faith. Isaiah had prophesied a virgin birth centuries before, somewhere between 740 and 701 BC, and this prophecy was fulfilled in Mary's conception of Jesus. The angel Gabriel brought the news to Mary, who, though free to say "no," chose instead to say "yes." Her courageous consent was a pivotal moment in God's divine plan, showcasing His deep respect for human free will as He invited Mary to participate in the salvation of the world.

Just as God had a unique and profound plan for Mary's life—one that included both immense suffering and overwhelming joy—He also has a plan for each of us. Your existence is no accident; it was intricately designed, just as Jesus's birth was divinely orchestrated. As the Lord declares through the prophet Jeremiah, *"Before I formed you in the womb I knew you, before you were born I dedicated you"* (Jeremiah 1:5). God, in His infinite wisdom, chose the precise time and place of your birth, the people who would accompany you, and the experiences that would shape your journey.

Like Jesus, who faced opposition and evil from the very beginning—from Herod's murderous intent to the agony of Gethsemane—you too will encounter challenges and trials. Yet, just as Jesus triumphed, you too can find strength and resilience through your faith. Remember the words of the Apostle Paul: *"We know that all things work for good for those who love God, who are called according to his purpose"* (Romans 8:28). This promise reassures us that no matter what we face, God's hand is guiding us towards a greater good.

Mary's life was a tapestry woven with threads of both joy and sorrow. She experienced the struggles of homelessness, the profound gift of motherhood, the simple pleasures of village life, the warmth of marriage, and the excruciating pain of witnessing her Son's suffering and death. In your journey, you too will encounter moments of indescribable joy, deep fulfillment, and profound sorrow. Yet, amid all these experiences, one gift will define and give your life meaning—your faith in God.

You have been chosen, as Peter reminds us, to be *"a chosen race, a royal priesthood, a holy nation, a people of his own"* (1 Peter 2:9). You are predestined, called, and justified, as Paul writes in Romans 8:30, to receive the same Holy Spirit that overshadowed Mary on the day of her Annunciation. Today, take a moment to offer a special prayer of thanksgiving, for God has granted you the extraordinary gift of carrying within you the living Christ. Just as Mary's "yes" brought salvation into the world, your own faith and trust in God's plan can bring His light to those around you.

Reflect on the Annunciation and, remember that God's plan for your life is as intentional and loving as His plan for Mary. Through your faith, you are called to participate in His ongoing work of redemption, carrying Christ within you and sharing His love with the world. Embrace this calling with the same courage and faith that Mary displayed, knowing that with God, all things are possible.

Lenten Reflection: Reflect on the fact that the same Holy Spirit that lived within Mary is living right now within you! Glory and praise to Jesus Christ.

Day 22

Wednesday of the Third Week of Lent

March 26, 2025

Deuteronomy 4:1, 5–9

Psalm 147

Matthew 5:17–19

"Do not think that I have come to abolish the law or the prophets. I have come not to abolish but to fulfill."

(Matthew 5:17)

Today's Gospel reading from Matthew can indeed be challenging to interpret. When Jesus declares, *"Do not think that I have come to abolish the law or the prophets. I have come not to abolish but to fulfill"* (Matthew 5:17), it raises the question: Why don't Christians follow all 613 commandments from the Old Testament, as devout Jews do? The key to understanding this lies in the word "fulfill."

Jesus emphasizes that *"not the smallest letter or the smallest part of a letter will pass from the law, until all things have taken place"* (Matthew 5:18). At first glance, this statement suggests that every aspect of the law remains in force. However, immediately after, Jesus introduces teachings that deepen and expand upon the law, such as when He says, *"You have heard it was said to your ancestors, 'You shall not kill; and whoever kills will be liable to judgment.' But I say to you, whoever is angry with his brother will be liable to judgment"* (Matthew 5:22). This indicates that Jesus is doing more than merely affirming the old law—He is transforming it.

To fully grasp what Jesus means by fulfilling the law, we need to recognize that He is pointing to a deeper spiritual reality. The law given in the Old Testament was a guide, but it was incomplete—no one could keep it perfectly. As noted in the Book of Acts, *"Why, then, are you putting God to the test by placing on the shoulders of the disciples a yoke that neither our ancestors nor we have been able to bear?"* (Acts 15:10). The law's fulfillment comes through Jesus, who perfectly embodies and accomplishes all that the law was meant to achieve.

When Jesus says on the Cross, *"It is finished"* (John 19:30), He signifies the completion of His mission and the fulfillment of the law. The tearing of the Temple curtain at that moment symbolizes the end of the old covenant, marked by ritual sacrifices and strict legal adherence, and the beginning of a new covenant, characterized by a law written on our hearts. This is the fulfillment of the prophecy in Jeremiah: *"I will place my law within them, and write it upon their hearts"* (Jeremiah 31:33).

For Christians, this new covenant is lived out through the indwelling of the Holy Spirit, who enables us to fulfill the law's true purpose. This purpose is summarized by Jesus in the commandments to love God with all our heart, soul, and mind, and to love our neighbor as ourselves (Matthew 22:37-40). We no longer need to master every detail of the law because the essence of the law—love—is inscribed on our hearts by the Spirit.

In this way, Jesus did not abolish the law but brought it to its fullest expression. The law's purpose is realized not through rigid adherence to rules but through the transformation of our hearts by love. As St. Paul writes, *"For the whole law is fulfilled in one statement, namely, 'You shall love your neighbor as yourself'"* (Galatians 5:14). This is the true fulfillment of the law that Jesus came to bring, a law that calls us to live in the fullness of God's love, joyfully and freely, reflecting the grace that has been given to us.

Let us embrace this call with hearts open to the Spirit, allowing God's love to guide every action and decision. In doing so, we live out the true purpose of the law, bringing light to the world and fulfilling God's will in our lives.

Lenten Reflection: Loving God and our neighbor is not a feeling, but a decision. The decision involves our behavior not our feelings. How can you decide to love God and neighbor today?

Day 23

Thursday of the Third Week of Lent

March 27, 2025

Jeremiah 7:23–28

Psalm 95:1–2, 6–9

Luke 11:14–23

"This rather is what I commanded them: Listen to my voice; then I will be your God and you shall be my people. Walk in all the ways that I command you, so that you may prosper. But they obeyed not, nor did they pay heed. They walked in the hardness of their evil hearts and turned their backs, not their faces, to me."

(Jeremiah 7:23–24)

The Bible readings today present a striking contrast: Israel during Jeremiah's time, stubbornly refusing to listen to God's voice, and the Pharisees in Jesus's audience, who accused Him of being an instrument of Beelzebub, the prince of demons. Ironically, the only beings in Jesus's crowd who truly recognized and obeyed Him were the demons possessing the mute man! Despite Jeremiah's prophetic warnings and Jesus's profound teachings, not everyone was moved.

Even after Jesus delivered His powerful teaching on the Eucharist—His flesh and blood—many disciples found it too difficult to accept and chose to walk away (John 6:58).

In our world today, particularly in Europe and the United States, we witness a similar trend: an increasing number of people are turning their backs on Jesus, much like those in Jeremiah's time who ignored God's call. It's not that they are actively rejecting Christ; rather, He simply isn't significant enough to warrant their attention. They pass Him by with indifference, His voice drowned out in the cacophony of modern life. To many, the voice of Christ is just one more among billions of others on platforms like YouTube and TikTok, easily ignored or dismissed with the flick of a finger. When confronted with anything related to Jesus, they simply change the channel.

We all know people who no longer listen to the voice of Jesus. Some have not outright rejected Him, but they have effectively silenced Him, removing His voice from their lives as easily as deleting an app from their iPhone. They aren't listening anymore. In moments like these, we must acknowledge that this is beyond our power to change. It is not within our human capacity to persuade or teach them into faith. The best we can do is entrust them to God's care and commit to prayer.

When the disciples faced a similar challenge and were unable to perform a particular miracle, they asked Jesus why their efforts had failed. Jesus responded, *"This kind can only come out through prayer"* (Mark 9:29). There is profound wisdom in this. The door to people's hearts has a knob that only they can turn from the inside. It is only through prayer that we invite God to knock gently, persistently, and lovingly at that door. Only He, dwelling within the hearts of those we care about, can open it.

As we journey through this Lenten season, reflecting on the stubbornness of Israel and the blindness of the Pharisees, let us also consider our role as intercessors. When words and reasoning fail, when the noise of the world drowns out the voice of Christ, our prayers become the most powerful tool we have. The Apostle Paul reminds us, *"Have no anxiety at all, but in everything, by prayer and petition, with thanksgiving, make your requests known to God"* (Philippians 4:6). Let us pray with unwavering faith, trusting that God's love is relentless and that He will continue to reach out to those who have turned away, gently calling them back to His embrace. Let us be steadfast in our prayers, confident that no soul is beyond the reach of God's mercy and grace. In His time, and by His will, those who have wandered may yet find their way back to the heart of the Father.

Lenten Reflection: Imagine the faces of people in your life who no longer demonstrate a profound love for Jesus. Lift them up before the Lord and imagine him laying his hand on their head. Imagine Jesus sending his Spirit into them. No words are necessary in this prayer beyond repeating the Name of Jesus.

Day 24

Friday of the Third Week of Lent

March 28, 2025

Hosea 14:2–10

Psalm 81:6–11, 14, 17

Mark 12:28–34

"The first is this: 'Hear, O Israel! The Lord our God is Lord alone! You shall love the Lord your God with all your heart, with all your soul, with all your mind, and with all your strength.' The second is this: 'You shall love your neighbor as yourself.' "

(Mark 12:29–31)

How is your love life? This may seem like a straightforward question, but within the context of faith, it delves deeply into the very core of who we are in relation to God and others. The two greatest commandments—loving God with all your heart and loving your neighbor as yourself—summarize our "love life" in the most profound way. At the heart of this is the concept of commitment. True love cannot exist without commitment; it is this commitment that elevates a relationship, infusing it with responsibility, dedication, and a sense of obligation.

When we say we are committed to God, it means far more than just professing belief. It means taking on the responsibility of nurturing our relationship with Him—through prayer, reflection, and integrating God into the fabric of our daily lives. This commitment demands that we actively seek His presence, listen to His voice, and align our actions with His will. Similarly, when we commit to others, we embrace the responsibility for their well-being, which includes caring for their spiritual journey. Jesus entrusted us with this responsibility when He commanded us to go into the world and share the Good News of His teachings.

The Christian understanding of God is deeply relational. God exists as a Trinity—Father, Son, and Holy Spirit—a perfect and eternal communion of love. If we are made in God's image and likeness, then our identity is also defined by our relationships with God and with one another. Jesus provides a clear definition of love in the Final Judgment scene in Matthew 25:31–45. Here, He asks if we have welcomed the stranger, fed the hungry, given drink to the thirsty, clothed the naked, cared for the ill, or visited the prisoner. These are not abstract concepts but concrete actions that manifest our love for our neighbor. In loving our neighbor, we demonstrate our love for God. As Jesus said, *"Whatever you did for one of these least brothers of mine, you did for me"* (Matthew 25:40).

God's understanding of love transcends mere emotion; it is an examination of how we live out our commitments and responsibilities to others. Christian love is fundamentally a decision—a deliberate choice to act in love, regardless of our feelings. Jesus's definition of love in the Gospels makes no mention of feelings because feelings can be fleeting and often beyond our control. You may not like everyone you encounter, and that is perfectly natural. But love, as Christ defines it, is about how we choose to treat others—how we decide to act in kindness, mercy, and compassion, even when we don't feel like it.

In this way, love becomes a reflection of our commitment to God and to the people around us. It is in our actions, our decisions, and our willingness to serve that we embody the love of Christ. As we reflect on our love life, let us ask ourselves: How committed are we to God? How committed are we to those around us? And how do these commitments manifest in our daily lives? By making love a conscious choice, rooted in commitment and responsibility, we align ourselves more closely with the heart of God, who is love itself.

Let us be encouraged by the words of 1 John 4:16: *"God is love, and whoever remains in love remains in God and God in him."* May this truth guide our actions and our hearts, leading us to live out our faith with love, compassion, and unwavering commitment to God and others.

Lenten Reflection: Think about the people you do not like. Some of these people may be public figures. How do you treat them? What needs to change?

Day 25

Saturday of the Third Week of Lent

March 29, 2025

Hosea 6:1–6

Psalm 51:3–4, 18–21

Luke 18:9–14

"But the tax collector stood off at a distance and would not even raise his eyes to heaven but beat his breast and prayed, 'O God, be merciful to me a sinner.' "

(Luke 18:13)

It is easy, when reading Jesus's parables, to fall into the trap of labeling the Pharisees as hypocritical, legalistic, and rigid, while viewing the poor as honest, empathetic, and loving. Take today's parable, for example. It seems to divide the world into two types of people: the good and the bad, the loving and the unloving. And, naturally, most of us would align ourselves with the tax collector, assuming that we are the ones who possess humility and sincerity. We like to think well of ourselves—at least, I know I do.

The problem with these labels is that they oversimplify the reality of who the Pharisees were. Many of them were genuinely good people who took Scripture seriously and earnestly tried to keep the commandments. The Pharisees were, in fact, the group that advocated for all men to learn the Torah, not just the Levites. Some among them believed that the Torah could be adapted to fit everyday life, allowing for a degree of flexibility in its observance. Many were also generous, giving far beyond the prescribed tithe of 10 percent to support those in need. On the other hand, tax collectors were not a monolithic group either. Some were simply trying to survive, earning a living in the only way they knew how, while others were indeed Roman collaborators who exploited their fellow Jews to enrich themselves.

The problem with dualistic thinking—dividing people into categories of "good" and "bad"—is that it fails to capture the complexity of human beings. There aren't just two types of people in the world. Instead, there are infinitely complex individuals, each trying to navigate the challenges of life as best they can. The truth is, we all carry within us the potential to be both the Pharisee and the humble tax collector. At different moments in our lives, we are both saint and sinner, capable of great good and, at times, of great failing.

In a time when our country feels more divided than ever, it is tempting to demonize those who hold opposing views, to blame them for the problems we see in society. But as followers of Jesus, we are called to a different standard. It's time for us to step back, take a breath, and recognize the humanity in each person. Goodness, reason, and love exist in everyone, though in varying degrees. Our task, as disciples of Christ, is to seek out the good in others, to name it, and to nurture it. As the Apostle Paul reminds us, *"Finally, brothers, whatever is true, whatever is honorable, whatever is just, whatever is pure, whatever is lovely, whatever is gracious, if there is any excellence . . . think about these things"* (Philippians 4:8–9).

Jesus himself emphasizes the importance of looking beyond mere appearances and labels when he says, *"Stop judging by appearances, but judge justly"* (John 7:24). This teaching reminds us that our judgments must be rooted in love, understanding, and a genuine desire to see others through the eyes of God.

By focusing on what is good, honorable, and true in others, we move beyond simplistic labels and embrace the richness of our shared humanity. We learn to see each person not as part of a binary system of right and wrong, but as a complex individual made in the image of God. In doing so, we foster understanding, compassion, and love—qualities that can heal divisions and build bridges where there were once walls. Let us commit ourselves to this path, seeking the good in everyone we encounter, and allowing Christ's love to guide our thoughts, words, and actions.

May we always remember that God's love is the lens through which we should view the world transforming our relationships and helping us to live out our calling as followers of Christ.

Lenten Reflection: When am I a Pharisee and when am I the tax collector? How do I waver between being both prideful and humble in my own life?

Day 26
Fourth Sunday of Lent

March 30, 2025

Joshua 5:9a, 10–11

2 Corinthians 5:17–21

Luke 15:1–3, 11–32

"My son, you are here with me always; everything I have is yours. But now we must celebrate and rejoice, because our brother was dead and has come to life again; he was lost and has been found."

(Luke 15:31–32)

In Luke 15, Jesus presents three parables about being lost: a sheep, a coin, and a son. These stories reveal how deeply interconnected we are as human beings. What is lost profoundly affects what remains, creating ripples of sorrow and longing in those left behind. The absence of the younger son, for instance, deeply impacts both the father and the older brother, leaving them emotionally adrift in their own home. This interconnectedness is beautifully highlighted at the end of each parable, where a joyful reunion calls together the community—friends, neighbors, and family— reminding us that we share in both the sorrows and the joys of one another. God has woven our relationships into the very fabric of our identity. Our connections with others are not just part of our lives; they define who we are.

Yet, throughout history, communities have often misunderstood this interconnectedness, viewing individuality as a threat rather than a strength. Too often, uniformity has been demanded as a condition for belonging. Those who are different—the Protestant in Catholic France, the Catholic in Protestant England, the transgender person in a Christian parish, or the Hasidic teenager wearing red—have been treated like outcasts, as if their uniqueness were a cancer to be excised. Kenneth Bailey writes of a Jewish custom during Jesus's time: if a Jewish son lost his inheritance among Gentiles and tried to return home, the community would smash a large pot in front of him, symbolically cutting him off from both family and community. This act declared him dead to all present, a message that there was no forgiveness for such a breach, and no possibility of coming home.

How could we, as Christians, have missed the heart of Jesus's message? Jesus welcomed, embraced, and celebrated individuality. If He could sit at the table with tax collectors, lepers, women, and adulteresses, how could we justify excluding anyone? By eating with sinners, Jesus willingly bore the shame before the community, offering a seat at the family table to those who had been cast out. He was undoing the division brought about by the original sin of Eden, which had broken our communion with both God and neighbor. His actions were revolutionary, challenging the norms of His time.

Ultimately, Jesus would take on the greatest shame of all when He embraced the cross. By descending to the lowest level of human experience—dying a criminal's death—He opened the way for all of us to rise with Him in the resurrection. As the Scriptures remind us, *"For the Son of Man has come to seek and to save what was lost"* (Luke 19:10). Satan seeks to break pots and shatter lives, but Jesus reveals the boundless mercy, love, and grace of our Father in heaven. He bore our shame so that we would not have to. He wants each of us home because it isn't truly home as long as our seat is empty.

Let us embrace the message of these parables, understanding that we are all connected in God's love. No matter how lost we may feel, there is always a place for us at the table. With open hearts, let us welcome others with the same love and mercy that Christ has shown us, knowing that in doing so, we bring a piece of heaven to earth.

Lenten Reflection: Who is not made to feel welcome in your family, your group, your church community? How might you work to change this?

Day 27

Monday of Fourth Week of Lent

March 31, 2025

Isaiah 65:17–21

Psalm 30

John 4:43–54

"Lo, I am about to create new heavens and a new earth; The things of the past shall not be remembered or come to mind. Instead, there shall always be rejoicing and happiness in what I create."

(Isaiah 65:17–18a)

When Jesus first encounters the royal official, He questions the man's motives. Has he come seeking signs and wonders, or is his faith genuine? Jesus resists being seen as a mere magician, performing miracles to prove His power. He challenges us to go beyond the superficial desire for signs and to seek a deeper relationship with Him. Even today, people demand proof: "Raise the dead, and then I'll believe." This recalls the story of the rich man who, after death, asks Abraham to send Lazarus back to warn his brothers of their fate. But Abraham responds, *"If they will not listen to Moses and the prophets, neither will they be persuaded if someone should rise from the dead"* (Luke 16:31). Indeed, someone has risen from the dead—Jesus. Yet, despite this ultimate miracle, faith is not merely about witnessing wonders; it is about trusting in the One who performs them.

The royal official's belief does not hinge on a miracle; it is already grounded in faith. He recognizes Jesus as the promised Messiah, the Christ. This faith, even before witnessing the miracle, is what heals. *"Faith is the realization of what is hope for and evidence of things not seen"* (Hebrews 11:1). Faith opens the door to eternal life, and it is this faith that Jesus calls each of us to embody. The healing of the official's son is not just a testament to Jesus's power; it is a revelation of the transformative nature of faith itself.

The purpose of St. John's Gospel signs is to reveal the true identity of Christ. These signs are not just miracles for the sake of awe but manifestations of who Jesus is—the Savior, the Son of God. Knowing Jesus as Savior is the essence of faith, and that faith transforms who we are in the world. It opens our hearts to the indwelling of the Holy Spirit, birthing us into a new way of being. With faith, Jesus moves from merely being an idea in the royal official's mind to being the center of his heart and spirit. This shift is what defines true discipleship—a life where Jesus is at the core of all we think, say, and do.

The story does not conclude with a celebration of the son's healing because the healing itself is not the ultimate focus. Instead, the parable ends with the man's entire household coming to faith. This illustrates that the true miracle is not just in the physical healing, but in the spiritual awakening that follows. The identity of Christ is the central truth, and the goal of each of the six signs in St. John's Gospel is to lead us to that faith. It is a faith that goes beyond the need for signs, resting instead on the deep, personal knowledge of Jesus as our Savior.

As we reflect on this passage, let us be reminded that true faith transforms not only individuals but entire households, communities, and ultimately, the world. "For where two or three are gathered together in my name, there am I in the midst of them" (Matthew 18:20). May our faith in Jesus, the Son of God, inspire us to be agents of transformation in the world, bringing His love and truth to those around us.

Lenten Reflection: What do you see in the world that tells you Jesus is the Son of God? How do you manage to maintain your faith without signs and wonders?

Day 28

Tuesday of Fourth Week of Lent

Ezekiel 47:1–9, 12

Psalm 46:2–3, 5–6, 8–9

John 5:1–16

"The sick man answered him, 'Sir, I have no one to put me into the pool when the water is stirred up; while I am on my way, someone else goes down there before me.' Jesus said to him, 'Rise, take up your mat, and walk.' "

(John 5:7–8)

The pool of Bethesda was the Lourdes of Jesus's day. Fed by hot springs, the water would occasionally bubble up, leading people to believe it held healing powers. For the Jews, water was the most powerful symbol of Messianic times. This is echoed in Ezekiel's prophecy that water would one day pour out from all four sides of the Temple, bringing fertility to the whole earth (Ezekiel 47:1–12). When we consider how the Gospel that began in Jerusalem has spread to every corner of the planet, we see Ezekiel's prophecy fulfilled in Jesus. Jesus is this Water of Life. The crippled man did not need to enter the pool because the Living Water was already speaking with him. Recall that Jesus had just identified Himself as the Living Water to the Samaritan woman at Jacob's well (John 4:10).

But Jesus, the Living Water, is so much more. He is the Word through whom all things came to be—the Creator Himself. While God created the world in six days and rested on the Sabbath, all Jews knew that life continued: babies were still born, rain still fell, and plants still grew. Clearly, God may have rested on the first Sabbath, but His divine work continued every day thereafter. Only God, as the Creator, could claim the right to work on the Sabbath, a right no human dared assume. Yet, when Jesus performed miracles on the Sabbath, He was claiming this divine right, a claim that was seen as blasphemous. The Pharisees' anger at Jesus reveals the gravity of His claim.

Jesus's declaration of being one with the Father was not just a statement—it was a profound claim to divinity, an assertion that those who heard Him found impossible to ignore. The Pharisees and Herodians even plotted Jesus's death after He healed a man with a withered hand on the Sabbath (Mark 3:6). Jesus seemed to be intentionally challenging their understanding of the Sabbath. It was on the Sabbath that He healed the crippled woman who could not stand erect (Luke 13:12). The blind beggar whom Jesus healed boldly professed Jesus as the promised Son of Man and worshiped Him (John 9:38). These acts were not just miracles; they were declarations of His divine authority, inviting all who witnessed them to see Jesus for who He truly was—God incarnate, the source of eternal life.

As Jesus says in John 5:24, *"Amen, amen, I say to you, whoever hears my word and believes in the one who sent me has eternal life and will not come to condemnation, but has passed from death to life."* This teaching emphasizes that the path to eternal life is through faith in Jesus and the Father who sent Him. The healing at the pool of Bethesda is not merely a story of physical restoration but a powerful reminder of the spiritual healing and life that Jesus offers to all who believe.

In this Lenten season, as we reflect on these miracles, let us deepen our faith in Jesus, the Living Water. May we recognize His divine authority in our lives and trust in His power to bring us from death to life. Just as the crippled man encountered Jesus and was made whole, so too can we encounter Him and be transformed. Let us embrace the life He offers, knowing that His grace is sufficient for every need, and His love is unending.

Lenten Reflection: Picture in your mind an image of Jesus from whose body is flowing a stream of light. Watch that light flow through people you want to pray for. No words are necessary with this prayer. The Lord knows your intentions.

Day 29

Wednesday of Fourth Week of Lent

April 2, 2025

Isaiah 49:8–15

Psalm 145:1–9, 13–14, 17–18

John 5:17–30

" 'My Father is at work until now, so I am at work.' For this reason the Jews tried all the more to kill him, because he not only broke the sabbath but he also called God his own father, making himself equal to God."

(John 5:17–18)

There is no doubt that Jesus claimed to be God's equal and, more than that, One with the Father in perfect communion. As such, Jesus will act as the ultimate judge at the end of time. He is the Son of Man, the giver of life, and the resurrection itself. Jesus holds the power to bestow immortality upon those He raises. He is the Lord of Time, the Alpha and the Omega, who transcends the boundaries of life and death: *"I am the resurrection and the life; whoever believes in me, even if he dies, will live, and everyone who lives and believes in me will never die"* (John 11:25-26).

Of all the gifts God has given us, time is perhaps the most precious—and it is slipping away with each passing moment. Death, the inevitable end of our earthly journey, brings anguish and torment beyond words. Grief seeps into our lives, casting a shadow even over moments of joy, peace, and hope. Yet, the promise of eternal life offers a comfort that surpasses all understanding. Knowing that we will one day be reunited with those we love infuses light into the darkest corners of our loneliness and despair. The hope for more time, for another embrace, another shared moment, is the ultimate yearning of the human heart.

It is to this deep, universal longing that God speaks when He says, *"Comfort, give comfort to my people, says your God. Speak tenderly to Jerusalem"* (Isaiah 40:1–2). Jesus Himself has reassured us that death is not the final word. He has gone to prepare a place for us and will return to take us to be with Him: *"Do not let your hearts be troubled. You have faith in God; have faith also in me. In my Father's house there are many dwelling places... I will come back again and take you to myself, so that where I am you also may be"* (John 14:1-3). *"Can a mother forget her infant, be without tenderness for the child of her womb? Even should she forget, I will never forget you. See, upon the palms of my hands I have written your name"* (Isaiah 49:15–16).

Without Jesus, life would be a fleeting journey with no meaning, no purpose. This world offers nothing that will last, nothing of ultimate value. Without Christ, virtues like faith, hope, and love would be dead ends, withering away like grass under the relentless sun. Among all the Gospels, St. John's is the clearest and most comforting voice to those who grieve, offering the profound reassurance that the last word no longer belongs to death but to Christ. He is God among us— Immanuel—who will make all things new. He will restore the aged, decayed body of the old, reunite the lips of loving spouses long separated by death, place infants once again in their mother's empty arms, and lift up from the gutters those who had been discarded by the world. This is the good news of the Gospel! May all those we cherish come to faith in Him and find the eternal life He promises.

Lenten Reflection: Among all those who have passed, who do you miss the most? Thank Jesus for his promise that you will see them again. And claim his peace. The Holy Spirit is with you.

Day 30

Thursday of Fourth Week of Lent

April 3, 2025

Exodus 32:7–14

Psalm 106:19–23

John 5:31–47

"Jesus said to him, 'I am the way and the truth and the life. No one comes to the Father except through me.' "

(John 14:6)

I had just settled into my first parish assignment as a new priest when I received an unexpected call requesting a meeting. Three people from a local church wanted to meet with me, the new priest, with the express purpose of "saving my soul." Fresh out of seminary, where the study of Scripture was still vivid in my mind, I felt confident and well-prepared for this encounter. In fact, I genuinely believed I could win them over. We met in my study, where my library was within arm's reach, a resource I was sure would bolster my arguments. They chose the topics, and the exchange remained respectful throughout. However, at every critical juncture where I presented what I knew to be indisputable historical or exegetical evidence supporting the Church's position, they immediately changed the subject. It dawned on me that no matter what I said, no matter how many authoritative texts I could open to support my case, it was irrelevant. They simply could not hear a word I was saying. It didn't matter what the topic was—truth seemed to have no bearing. Historical facts, carefully researched and documented, were dismissed out of hand. Their minds were fixed, unchangeable, and closed to any possibility of new understanding.

Jesus must have experienced this same frustration with the Pharisees. According to Jewish tradition, the testimony of two or three witnesses was sufficient to establish the truth (Deuteronomy 19:15). Jesus provided the Pharisees with multiple witnesses to verify His identity: (1) John the Baptist, (2) His miracles (works), (3) the testimony of the Father (Luke 3:22), (4) the witness of Scripture, and (5) the testimony of Moses (Deuteronomy 18:15). Despite this overwhelming evidence, the truth didn't matter to them—they simply were not listening.

Today, regardless of political affiliation, many people in the United States feel that those on the opposing side are willfully blind to the truth. Historical facts, analytical data, scientific evidence, and professional studies are often dismissed without even a moment of genuine reflection. It seems there is no persuading the other side, no breaking through the wall of preconceived notions and biases. This phenomenon, while perplexing, is nothing new. Yet, the consequences of dismissing truth are enormous, not just for individuals but for society as a whole. If we continue to ignore the truth, the future of our nation is at great risk—potentially catastrophic.

However, as dire as these political consequences may be, they pale in comparison to the consequences of dismissing Christ. Jesus is not just another figure in history; He is not merely another politician or teacher. Jesus is the truth incarnate, the living embodiment of God's Word. Ignoring or rejecting Him has eternal consequences, far beyond the temporal challenges of our world. As Scripture reminds us, *"Jesus said to him, 'I am the way and the truth and the life. No one comes to the Father except through me'"* (John 14:6). Ignoring or rejecting Him has eternal consequences, far beyond the temporal challenges of our world. Jesus is the only key to escaping the finality of death, the only way to truly live.

As we navigate the complexities of life and the challenges of our times, we must remember that it is only in embracing the truth of Christ that we find our true path forward—both in this life and the life to come.

Lenten Reflection: Take a moment to consider the fact that millions of Americans who disagree with your politics can't all be completely wrong. Give the Holy Spirit a moment to speak to your heart and try to LISTEN.

Day 31
Friday of Fourth Week of Lent

April 4, 2025

Wisdom 2:1a, 12–22

Psalm 34:19–23

John 7:1–2, 10, 25–30

"They who said among themselves, thinking not aright:

. . .

'Let us beset the just one, because he is obnoxious to us;
he sets himself against our doings, Reproaches us for
transgressions of the law and charges us with violations of our
training. . . .

Let us condemn him to a shameful death; for according to
his own words, God will take care of him."

(Wisdom 2:1,12, 20)

Have you ever found yourself in a situation where someone has decided they don't like you and seems to hang on every word you say, just waiting for you to slip up? Or perhaps you've experienced the tension of someone scrutinizing your every action, eager to twist it into something negative? When people make up their minds to dislike you, it can feel as though everything you do or say is under a microscope, needing constant

106

defense. It's as if their brain flips a switch, erasing any history of good intentions and focusing solely on the negative. This phenomenon is strikingly evident during times of conflict, like when workers go on strike and a few decide to keep working. Lifelong friendships can evaporate in mere hours, replaced by anger and resentment. You may have seen this same dynamic play out in recent years in the United States if you've ventured into the treacherous waters of political discussion with friends or family. Once you're labeled as one of "them," it feels like nothing you say or do can be viewed positively.

Psychologists have a term for this phenomenon: cognitive immunization. It means being immune to reality, to facts. In this state, your beliefs are impervious to being challenged by the truth, and no amount of contradictory evidence can change your mind. For those who have decided to dislike you, it doesn't matter what you do or say; you're still the enemy, and your intentions will always be seen as corrupt. When truth, goodness, and kindness no longer have an impact, we encounter something deeper and more troubling— what the Bible calls evil. By its very nature, evil is irrational.

As we approach Good Friday, we see all the characters in the story of Jesus taking their places, ready to act when the signal is given. Jesus has been labeled the enemy, and in the minds of those who oppose Him,

He must die. No amount of miracles, acts of forgiveness, compassion, or even walking on water and feeding five thousand could change their hardened hearts. The hour of evil had arrived.

In times like these, Jesus shows us the way. He goes to the Father in prayer, seeking strength and peace. This is where we must go as well. Let the Holy Spirit within you bring you before the Father in the name of Jesus, and place your life in God's hands. In doing so, claim the peace of Christ, knowing that your story is written by God Himself. As Jesus reminds us, *"In the world you will have trouble, but take courage, I have conquered the world"* (John 16:33). Evil did not have the last word in the life of Jesus, and it will not have the last word in your life either.

In the face of adversity, remember that God's plan for you is greater than any opposition you may encounter. Trust in His promise, and find comfort in the knowledge that His love and truth will ultimately prevail.

Lenten Reflection: Can you think of anyone or any group who is experiencing what was just described—the hour of evil? Will you take a moment and pray for them?

Day 32

Saturday of Fourth Week of Lent

April 5, 2025

Jeremiah 11:18–20

Psalm 7:2–3, 9–12

John 7:40–53

"Yet I, like a trusting lamb led to slaughter, had not realized that they were hatching plots against me: 'Let us destroy the tree in its vigor; let us cut him off from the land of the living, so that his name will be spoken no more.' "

(Jeremiah 11:19)

I do not know Jesus today in my 70s the way I knew Christ when I was ordained in my 20s. It's not just my thinking that has changed—my feelings have evolved as well. The truth is, my thoughts and emotions about nearly everything have shifted over the years. One of my greatest regrets in life is that, in my early years, I taught religion to children as though the information was more important than the experience of Jesus. If I had the chance to do it over, I would set aside the tests and textbooks and instead invite the children to truly encounter the person of Jesus, to experience His love, and perhaps to fall in love with Him as their Savior and friend. For when you journey through life with Jesus as your constant companion, expect everything to change. And it is precisely because I am a different person now that I can look back with a sense of regret, but also with a deeper understanding.

Scripture is filled with stories of people whose lives were transformed through their encounters with Jesus, showing us that change is a natural part of our spiritual journey. Take the man born blind, for instance. He was healed by Jesus, and as his story unfolds, so does his understanding of who Jesus is. At first, he simply sees Jesus as a man. Later, he acknowledges Jesus as a prophet. By the end of the story, when Jesus asks him if he believes in the Son of Man, he calls Jesus "Lord" and worships Him (John 9:38). His journey is one of growing faith and deepening relationship, illustrating how our perception of Christ can evolve over time.

Nicodemus, too, undergoes a significant transformation in his understanding of Jesus. We encounter him three times in the Gospel, and each time, his relationship with Jesus deepens. Initially, Nicodemus approaches Jesus at night, hesitant and perhaps fearful of being seen by his peers. In today's passage, we see Nicodemus stepping into the light, openly questioning and defending Jesus, even if only cautiously. By the end of the Gospel, Nicodemus stands beneath the Cross, a witness to the ultimate sacrifice, seemingly a committed disciple who has journeyed from curiosity to conviction.

Of course, this journey of faith can also take a different path. Some who once followed Christ with fervor have drifted away, becoming some of the most vocal critics of Jesus and His people. As children, they may have embraced the divinity of Christ with innocent faith, but as adults, they come to view it as mere historical fiction, disillusioned by what they once believed.

Yet, even in these stories of doubt and departure, there is hope. The beauty of our relationship with Jesus is that it is never too late to return, to rediscover His love, and to reignite our faith. Jesus never stops inviting us to walk with Him, no matter where we are on our journey. Whether we find ourselves growing closer to Him or drifting away, His arms remain open, ready to welcome us back. As the Psalmist reminds us, *"The Lord is close to the brokenhearted, saves those who are crushed"* (Psalm 34:18).

As we reflect on our own spiritual journeys, let us be encouraged that change is not something to fear but to embrace. Each step we take, each question we ask, and each experience we encounter brings us closer to the heart of Christ. And as we grow in our understanding and love for Him, we can find peace in knowing that He walks with us every step of the way, guiding us toward the fullness of life in Him.

Remember, it's not about how we started or where we've been—it's about where we're going, and with Jesus as our guide, the destination is always one of hope, renewal, and everlasting love.

Lenten Reflection: You are still here at the side of Jesus walking through your life. Has your understanding and faith in Jesus changed since your journey began? Do you love Jesus differently now after having walked awhile? Talk to Him about it.

Day 33
Fifth Sunday of Lent

April 6, 2025

Isaiah 43:16–21

Psalm 126:1–6

Philippians 3:8–14

John 8:1–11

"Jesus straightened up and said to her, 'Woman, where are they? Has no one condemned you?' She replied, 'No one, sir.' Then Jesus said, 'Neither do I condemn you. Go, [and] from now on do not sin anymore.' "

(John 8:10)

Most of the sermons I've preached over the years on this Gospel have focused on the importance of not judging others when they sin. The message has been to love the sinner without qualification, regardless of their choices, and to leave the judging to God. In essence, these sermons have placed my listeners among the crowd standing before the adulteress, hearing Jesus's call not to cast stones.

Today, I'd like to invite you to see this story from a different perspective. Imagine, for a moment, that you are the woman caught in adultery. More specifically, you are the one in the story who has committed the sin. What are some of the things you deeply regret? These might be actions you took or opportunities you let slip by. These sins, these mistakes, can weigh heavily on us, casting a shadow over our hearts, no matter how much time has passed.

Often, we are harder on ourselves than any crowd could ever be. We condemn ourselves for countless things—failing to visit someone in their time of need, neglecting to offer help when we could have, staying away from a nursing home, an unemployed relative, or a cousin who was incarcerated. Perhaps we have wished for the end of suffering for someone we love or harbored resentment towards a sibling or parent, withholding love as a form of punishment. We may hold onto wounds, nursing them instead of letting them heal, or regret giving up on a relationship or marriage too soon. Some of us have made material things a priority, causing rifts in our relationships, or have shared gossip with the intent to damage another's reputation. Indifference to the suffering around us, being too self-absorbed, or mistakes with money or our appearance—these, too, can fill us with guilt. We may even struggle to let go of anger or shame, despite having sought forgiveness in the Sacrament of Reconciliation.

But today, I want you to place yourself in the shoes of that woman standing in the midst of the crowd, with stones poised to be thrown at you. You know that part of you might even join in because a part of you believes you deserve to be punished. Now, hear Jesus speak these transformative words to you: "I do not condemn you. I love you just as you are. Leave the guilt, the shame, and the shadow here at My feet and go home. Take My peace with you. Receive My Holy Spirit, the Comforter. Enough already! Enough! I command you: Be free of the past. Live!"

As you stand there, imagine the weight of those stones being lifted, not by the hands of others, but by the mercy of Christ. The stones that could have crushed you are now laid down at His feet. His words are not just an absolution; they are an invitation to a new beginning. Jesus doesn't just forgive—He restores, He renews, and He sets us free. As Paul writes in Romans 8:1, *"There is no condemnation for those who are in Christ Jesus."* Today, let His love wash over you, and allow yourself to walk away from the crowd, not with the burden of the past, but with the light of His grace guiding your steps.

Embrace this freedom. Live in the fullness of the life He offers. Remember, Jesus's love for you is unchanging, His mercy is unending, and His desire for you is to walk in peace and joy. Let go of the past and step into the life He has prepared for you, a life of grace, forgiveness, and new beginnings.

Lenten Reflection: Make a decision right now that you will let go of whatever torments you and steals your inner peace. Give

the past to Jesus and claim the freedom he offers in his Spirit.
Accept Jesus's forgiveness and welcome the Holy Spirit to begin a
new life.

Day 34
Monday of the Fifth Week of Lent

April 7, 2025

Daniel 13:41–62

Psalm 23:1–6

John 8:12–20

"I am the light of the world. Whoever follows me will not walk in darkness, but will have the light of life."

(John 8:12)

"I am the light of the world." Notice that Jesus does not say, "I am a light." He boldly declares, "I am the light." This claim of exclusivity is profound and undeniable. Jesus positions Himself as the one true light, a beacon unmatched by any other. There are no other legitimate lights before God—Jesus is the first, the authentic, the foundational. Anything else that presents itself as a light is nothing more than a cheap imitation. Every human being is called on a journey that is predestined to end in the Kingdom of God. Just as every journey to a specific destination requires a map, Jesus is that map, the light that illuminates the way to life itself (John 8:12). Though other so-called "lights" may appear, offering to

117

guide us, and though many may choose to follow them, Jesus remains the only true light that leads to the Father. *"No one comes to the Father except through me"* (John 14:6).

In the early days of Christianity, believers were known as "the people of the Way," a name derived from Jesus's declaration in John 14:6: *"I am the way."* These early Christians were easily recognizable because their lives were distinctly different from those around them. The voice of the Creator guided each step they took and influenced every decision they made on their journey. Their actions, their choices, and their way of living were all reflections of the teachings of Jesus. They stood apart, not because they sought to be different, but because they followed the light of Christ so closely that it set them on a path uniquely defined by His truth and love.

In contrast, the world offers many gods, each claiming to provide directions for how life should be lived. From self-help gurus to false prophets, countless voices promise fulfillment and destinations that ultimately fall short of the truth. But Jesus is far more than just a guide or shepherd through life (John 10:14). He is the gate through which we enter at the journey's end, the door that opens to eternal life (John 10:7). In His very person, He embodies the resurrection and the life (John 11:25). The Lord alone covers every aspect of our journey, offering an all-inclusive package: peace in this world and unending life in the next. *"For God did not send his Son into the world to condemn the world, but that the world might be saved through him"* (John 3:17). No other offer can compare—there has never been, nor will there ever be, a better offer!

As we walk through life, we are constantly faced with choices about which light to follow. But when we choose Jesus, we are choosing the only light that leads to true fulfillment and eternal joy. His light dispels the darkness of our fears, doubts, and uncertainties, guiding us with a sure and steady hand. Let us embrace this light, let it illuminate our paths, and lead us to the fullness of life that only He can provide. Remember, the journey with Christ is one of purpose, peace, and unparalleled promise. With Jesus as our light, we will always find our way home to the Father.

Lenten Reflection: How might I learn more about the Way of Jesus? How do I put into practice what I hear?

Day 35
Tuesday of the Fifth Week of Lent

April 8, 2025

Numbers 21:4–9

Psalm 102:2–3, 16–21

John 8:21–30

"When you lift up the Son of Man, then you will realize that I AM, and that I do nothing on my own, but I say only what the Father taught me."

(John 8:28)

Today's Gospel from John takes us back to the time of Moses, around 1400 BC, when Israel had left Egypt and was journeying through the desert toward the Promised Land. As the journey dragged on, the people's faith began to falter, and they started to grumble: *"We are disgusted with this wretched food!"* (Numbers 21:5). Instead of expressing gratitude for God's provision, they fixated on what they lacked, allowing resentment and bitterness to take root in their hearts. Their grumbling echoed the sin of Adam and Eve, who, despite having everything, desired more. In response, God allowed Saraph serpents to invade the camp, biting and killing many. In desperation, the people turned to Moses for help.

Moses brought their plea before the Lord, who instructed him to mount a bronze serpent on a pole and lift it up. Those who looked upon the bronze serpent and placed their trust in God were healed (Numbers 21:4–9). St. John makes a profound connection between this event and the crucifixion of Christ: *"Just as Moses lifted up the serpent in the desert, so must the Son of Man be lifted up, so that everyone who believes in him may have eternal life"* (John 3:14–15). This parallel emphasizes the transformative power of faith.

The bronze serpent that Moses lifted before Israel restored their faith and granted them more time on earth—perhaps ten, thirty, or fifty more years. However, they all eventually faced death. In contrast, Christ, lifted up on the cross, offers something far greater: eternal life to all who believe and trust in Him. Jesus is much more than Moses could have imagined. He is the One who was with the Father in the burning bush, before whom Moses knelt and worshiped. Jesus is the pillar of fire and cloud that led the Israelites out of Egypt. He is the living water that flowed from the rock to quench the thirst of the Jews in the desert. He is the divine hand that provided manna from heaven when Israel was hungry.

Jesus is the Great I AM, without beginning or end, immortal, the very Word through whom all things were created. He is the Lord of Life, offering resurrection and eternal life to all who believe. Jesus is not just someone who existed before Abraham; He is One with the I AM of Sinai, who made the Temple holy by His Spirit. In Jesus, we find the fulfillment of every promise, the answer to every need, and the source of everlasting life.

As we reflect on these profound truths, let us lift our eyes to Christ, just as the Israelites looked upon the bronze serpent. Let us place our trust in Him, knowing that He is the source of our salvation and the one who offers us life beyond this world. In the midst of our own struggles and challenges, may we find hope and strength in the One who was lifted up for our sake. Jesus invites us to look to Him, to trust in His love and mercy, and to embrace the eternal life He offers. As the psalmist declares, *"The Lord is my light and my salvation; whom should I fear? The Lord is my life's refuge; of whom should I be afraid?"* (Psalm 27:1). In Him, we are renewed, restored, and made whole.

Lenten Reflection: Jesus has promised to go ahead and prepare a place for each of us, and then return to take us with him. How does this bring you comfort? Who are you waiting to see again?

Day 36

Wednesday of the Fifth
Week of Lent

April 9, 2025

Daniel 3:14–20, 91–92, 95.

Daniel 3:52–56

John 8:31–42

"If you remain in my word, you will truly be my disciples, and you will know the truth, and the truth will set you free."

(John 8:31–32)

Daniel's great story of Shadrach, Meshach, and Abednego speaks to the profound price that must be paid by those who choose to serve the God of Abraham. These three faithful brothers were thrown into a white-hot furnace for refusing to deny their God and worship King Nebuchadnezzar. Their faith had a cost, and they willingly paid it, even with their lives. In the midst of their trial, an angel of the Lord joined them in the flames, serving as a divine witness that God rewards such unwavering fidelity. Imagine the intense love these brothers had for God—a love so deep that they were willing to endure unimaginable torture. The irony in this story is striking: the three prisoners are, in fact, the only ones who are truly free.

As we approach Good Friday, we remember when Christ paid the ultimate price for our faith by dying on the Cross. After Jesus's death, an angel was also seen at the tomb, bearing witness to His great sacrifice. Like the brothers in Daniel, this is first and foremost a story of love before it is a story of sacrifice—a love so profound that it will pay any price for the beloved. The irony continues, for it is Jesus—not Pilate, not Herod, not the Romans, nor the Pharisee mob—who remains free, even as He is held as a prisoner.

Many in today's world view Christianity as something that chains the mind, imprisoning the spirit with bars of Scripture that stifle life and freedom. But we who have received the Holy Spirit know how truly ironic that perception is, for Christ and His teachings have made us free. We are free from fear, for Christ has given us a peace the world cannot comprehend. We no longer need to fear death. Jesus said, *"I am the resurrection and the life; whoever believes in me, even if he dies, will live"* (John 11:25). We are free from the chains of materialism, knowing that this world is passing away. We are free from resentment, revenge, and hatred, for we have embraced the transformative power of love. We have willingly entered the white-hot furnace by forgiving even our enemies and doing good to those who would harm us. We are free from the hunger for power, for true power belongs to those who choose to serve with humility and grace.

Christ has come to earth with the good news from the Father, a message that turns the values of this world upside down and inside out. *"Blessed are the poor in spirit, for theirs is the kingdom of heaven... Blessed are those who hunger and thirst for righteousness, for they will be satisfied"* (Matthew 5:3, 6). Jesus is Lord. Jesus is our Savior. And in Him, we find our ultimate freedom. We are free! Amen.

Lenten Reflection: How has your faith in Jesus set your spirit free? What chains used to hold you bound that have been broken by Christ?

Day 37

Thursday of the Fifth Week of Lent

April 10, 2025

Genesis 17:3–9

Psalm 105:4–9

John 8:51–59

"Jesus said to them, 'Amen, amen, I say to you, before Abraham came to be, I AM.' So they picked up stones to throw at him; but Jesus hid and went out of the temple area."

(John 8:58–59)

Depending on how you choose to count them, there are seven or eight "I AM" statements in John's Gospel. These "I AM" statements are not to be taken lightly! With each declaration, Christ is making an unequivocal identification between Himself and the Father in heaven. It was God on Mount Sinai who revealed Himself to Moses with the profound words, "I AM Who I Am." In ancient times, knowing the name of a god was believed to grant humans the power to summon that deity into their presence and compel it to listen to their pleas. However, the God of Israel, the one true Creator, would not permit such a sacrilege.

Humans cannot presume to wield power over the divine unless the Creator Himself chooses to bestow it. The term "I AM," represented by the tetragrammaton and later translated as "Yahweh" or "Jehovah," is not merely a name but a powerful statement of existence. God is "I AM," without beginning, existing outside the boundaries of time, immortal, and the Creator of all that is. Every time Jesus uses these words, "I AM," in reference to Himself, He is boldly claiming to be one with the Father, making Himself equal with God. The people of His time understood this, for the punishment prescribed by the law for such blasphemy was death by stoning, which is why they responded by picking up stones.

The implications of Jesus's divinity are profound and life-changing. If Jesus is indeed King, then the teachings of Jesus carry immense power, and every word He spoke is true. Jesus truly holds the key to salvation, the only lifeboat off this sinking ship we call earth. He is the gate through which we enter God's eternal Kingdom. Jesus is the Lamb seated on the throne of heaven, surrounded by countless hosts of angels and saints. And here's the most awe-inspiring truth: Jesus, in all His divine glory, is here by your side, listening to your every thought, enraptured by your presence. This God, whom the entire universe cannot contain, loves you deeply and intimately. Yes, He loves you so much that He took on physical form and came to earth in search of you. He desires your friendship so profoundly that what He once withheld from Israel on Mount Sinai, He now offers to you freely. Say His Name—Jesus. He, the Lord and Creator of all the universe, has promised to never leave your side.

As the psalmist declares, *"The Lord is my light and my salvation; whom should I fear? The Lord is my life's refuge; of whom should I be afraid?"* (Psalm 27:1). This assurance is the bedrock of our faith, reminding us that Jesus, the "I AM," is our constant protector and guide.

There's a powerful story told of Methodist Episcopal Bishop Warren Candler. As he lay on his deathbed, a friend asked him whether he was afraid. The friend inquired, "Please tell me frankly, do you fear crossing over the river of death?" Candler, with unwavering faith, replied, "Why, I belong to a Father who owns the land on both sides of the river."

This story beautifully captures the essence of our faith. Just as Bishop Candler had complete confidence in God's sovereignty over both life and death, we too can trust in Jesus, the "I AM," who has claimed us as His own. No matter where life's journey takes us— through trials, uncertainties, or even to the brink of death—we can rest assured that we belong to a God who holds all things in His hands. Jesus is not only our guide in this life but also our gateway to eternal life. With Him by our side, we can face any challenge, any fear, knowing that His love will carry us through. We are never alone, for Jesus is with us, now and forever. Amen.

Lenten Reflection: Angels kneel when the Name of Jesus is spoken. Sit quietly, be silent, listen to your breathing. Whisper his Name. Jesus. Jesus. Jesus is Lord.

Day 38
Friday of the Fifth Week of Lent

April 11, 2025

Jeremiah 20:10–13

Psalm 18:2–7

John 10:31–42

"If I do not perform my Father's works, do not believe me; but if I perform them, even if you do not believe me, believe the works, so that you may realize (and understand) that the Father is in me and I am in the Father."

(John 10:37–38)

One of the "works" Jesus refers to in John 10 is His miracles, or signs. In the chapter preceding today's Gospel, Jesus has just healed a blind man. However, the physical healing is not the most significant part of the story. The true miracle lies in the spiritual healing that unfolds. Initially, the man healed of his physical blindness sees Jesus as merely a "man" standing before him. But as the Spirit continues to lift his spiritual blindness, he begins to understand that Jesus is more than just an ordinary man—He is a prophet. By the end of the story, the man recognizes Christ as the Promised Son of Man and worships Him. As his spiritual sight is restored, the blindness of the Pharisees becomes increasingly severe, to the point where they want Jesus dead. To them, killing Him would be a service, for they believe He is either insane or possessed (John 10:19-21).

Where has the teaching of Jesus taken you? Is your spiritual blindness being lifted? Is your faith in Jesus as the Son of God clearer today than it was ten years ago? Do you find that your love for Jesus has deepened over time? Just as plants need regular watering and fertilizing to grow and thrive, our spiritual lives require nourishment. Reading Scripture and participating in the Eucharist are vital practices that nurture our faith and deepen our communion with the Spirit. The more we come to know Christ, the more our love for Him grows.

Jesus is the gatekeeper who deeply cares for His sheep. It is He who seeks out the blind man, not the other way around. The Good Shepherd searches for the lost sheep, while the Pharisees, in their spiritual blindness, show no concern for the man who has been healed. They act like hired hands who do not own the sheep and thus abandon them. The story concludes with the Pharisees casting the man out, further revealing their lack of true compassion.

In today's Gospel, Jesus challenges us to reflect on whether we can see His works and His presence in the world around us. Are we being healed of the spiritual blindness that afflicts all humankind? Can we, with all honesty, say that we have witnessed enough beauty, love, kindness, and goodness in the world to know with every fiber of our being that Jesus is here among us, always working His miracles, loving in and through His followers? As Scripture reminds us, *"For God, who said, 'Let light shine out of darkness,' has shone in our hearts to bring to light the knowledge of the glory of God on the face of [Jesus] Christ"* (2 Corinthians 4:6). Can we bear witness to the truth that Jesus is risen? He is Lord! Has your spiritual blindness been healed?

As you continue your journey with Christ, may your eyes be opened to the countless ways He reveals Himself in your life. Each day, may you grow in the certainty that Jesus is alive, working in and through you, offering His love, grace, and healing to the world. Let us rejoice in the truth that our blindness is being lifted, and with hearts full of faith, proclaim that Jesus is Lord—now and forever. Amen.

Lenten Reflection: Everything in your life depends on your relationship with the Lord. Make a decision that you are going to take efforts to grow in the Spirit.

Day 39

Saturday of the Fifth Week of Lent

April 12, 2025

Ezekiel 37:21–28

Psalm 31:10–13

John 11:45–56

"You know nothing, nor do you consider that it is better for you that one man should die instead of the people, so that the whole nation may not perish."

(John 11:49b–50)

We often group all the authority figures involved in the death of Jesus—Herod Antipas, Pontius Pilate, and Caiaphas—together in terms of responsibility. Each one had the power to save Jesus, yet none intervened to stop the events that led to His execution. However, when we delve deeper into the details, we may find ourselves more sympathetic to their positions. Take Caiaphas, for instance. In today's Gospel, his reasoning seems logical: *"It is better for you that one man should die instead of the people, so that the whole nation may not perish"* (John 11:50). The Bible does not portray these words as the ruminations of a selfish man, but rather as a prophecy that Jesus *"was going to die for the nation"* (John 11:51). If this was indeed a true prophecy, does it not suggest that the Spirit of God was at work in Caiaphas's mind?

Consider Caiaphas's dilemma. Is it justifiable to sacrifice one innocent person if it means saving many—perhaps even millions? Would that make it a righteous act to take one life to preserve countless others? These are profound moral quandaries. If you could kill Hitler to save millions of Jews, or Putin to save Ukrainians, would that be considered a good deed? The value of an individual life is a complex issue, and arguments can be made on both sides depending on whose life is at stake and countless other factors. While I cannot explore all these complexities here, I simply want to highlight that there are often two sides to every story. Perhaps even Caiaphas, Herod, and Pontius Pilate had moments of good intentions within their hearts.

Yet, when we reflect on our Bible readings today, one point stands out clearly: Jesus seems to elevate the value of an individual life over the collective whole. The shepherd risks the safety of the entire flock to find the one lost sheep. The life of one adulteress was worth more to Jesus than His own credibility and standing with the Pharisees. Befriending a single tax collector was more important than the opinions of the majority. Including a person He knew would betray Him in His inner circle was worth the risk to Jesus, even at the cost of His safety and life. Healing ten lepers was significant, even though only one returned to give thanks.

This perspective sheds light on one of the most painful scandals in the history of the Church: the abuse of individuals in the name of protecting the institution. The true tragedy is that the lives of these innocent individuals were sacrificed for the perceived good of the whole. Instead of risking the public scandal that would have erupted if the Church had reported every crime, Church authorities chose to protect the institution's image, sacrificing each individual child or adult victim in the process. They prioritized the appearance of holiness over the reality of profound brokenness within. What, then, is the life of an individual worth to an organization? In these instances of abuse, it seems the answer was far too little.

But as we reflect on these difficult truths, let us also find hope and encouragement in the example of Jesus. His life and teachings remind us that every individual life has infinite value. Jesus did not sacrifice the one for the many; rather, He sought out the lost, the broken, and the outcast, valuing each person as a precious child of God. As the Psalmist declares, *"You formed my inmost being; you knit me in my mother's womb. I praise you, so wonderfully you have made me"* (Psalm 139:13-14). In our own lives, let us strive to follow His example, elevating the worth of each person we encounter, standing up for those who are vulnerable, and recognizing that every life matters deeply to God. In doing so, we honor the true spirit of Christ's message—one of love, compassion, and the infinite worth of every soul. Amen.

Lenten Reflection: By offering benefits to illegal immigrants, is it right to sacrifice the needs of citizens whose families have been in the United States for centuries? Are illegal immigrants worth the financial well-being of the whole country? Are addicts and prisoners worth the public expense? Is an unborn child worth the long-term goals of a young, intelligent woman who wants a career, a home, and a family in the future? What is the value of an individual over the group?

Day 40

Palm Sunday of the Lord's Passion

April 13, 2025

Isaiah 50:4–7

Psalm 22

Philippians 2:6–11

Luke 22:14–23:56

"After withdrawing about a stone's throw from them and kneeling, he prayed, saying, 'Father, if you are willing, take this cup away from me; still, not my will but yours be done.'"

(Luke 22:41–42)

Our liturgical journey begins today with the triumphal entry of Jesus into Jerusalem. The crowd, waving palm branches and shouting "Hosanna" (which means "Save us, Lord"), was reenacting the triumphal entry of two warriors into Jerusalem, one in 164 BC and another in 141 BC. These warriors had delivered the people from foreign armies and false gods. Passover, the religious holiday that celebrated yet another great liberation— the exodus from Egyptian slavery—was also in full swing. Here, three political victories and three religious feasts are intertwined, and Jesus chooses this powerful moment to enter Jerusalem. With crowds that may have numbered close to two million, the tension was palpable. One spark could ignite a fire that could consume the entire nation.

As we join today's crowd with our own cries of "Save us, Lord," we must also remember that it is with these same voices that we will cry out "Crucify Him" on Friday. We are part of the human condition that crucified Christ. It is for our sins that He suffered and died. This week, take a deep and honest look at your life and ask yourself if you have truly worked to build the Kingdom that Jesus announced. Have you loved as Jesus modeled? Have you forgiven as He asked us to?

This week, immerse yourself not only in the collective voice of the crowd but also in the minds and hearts of the individual characters we encounter in the Gospel stories. Empathize with Caiaphas, who believed he was saving the nation; with Judas, who longed for a political victory and freedom; with Peter, who was gripped by fear; with Mary, who bore the agony of watching her Son be crucified; with John, who held Mary as she wept; and with Nicodemus, who offered his burial chamber out of reverence. If possible, watch some of the series *The Chosen* with your family. Step beyond being an observer—become a participant. Make this journey through Holy Week personal. Let it be your own.

There are fifty-two weeks in a year. Consider dedicating just this one week back to God by following Jesus through the profound events of Holy Week, culminating on Easter Sunday. Take time to go online and research the significance of Holy Thursday, Good Friday, and the Easter Vigil so that you can prepare yourself to truly join Jesus in His journey. This week is what many refer to as a "thin place," where the spiritual and physical worlds draw near, and the Spirit seems to cross over into our hearts and minds in moments of awe and wonder. It is a sacred opportunity to commune deeply with God.

As you walk this sacred path, let it transform you. Allow the profound events of this week to deepen your faith, renew your spirit, and fill you with a greater understanding of Christ's immeasurable love. *"Come to me, all you who labor and are burdened, and I will give you rest"* (Matthew 11:28). Let this be a time of reflection, renewal, and recommitment to living out the Gospel in your daily life. As you reach Easter Sunday, may you do so with a heart filled with gratitude, a spirit renewed by grace, and a voice ready to proclaim, "He is risen!" This is your journey. Embrace it fully, and let it lead you closer to the heart of God.

Lenten Reflection: We are not playacting this week as if our liturgies were theater. Liturgy is not pretend. We enter the sacred space where the walls of time collapse and the past is made present. Let your faith lead you into the very life of the Spirit.

Day 41
Monday of Holy Week

April 14, 2025

Isaiah 42:1–7

Psalm 27:1–3, 13–14

John 12:1–11

"Then Judas the Iscariot, one (of) his disciples, and the one who would betray him, said, 'Why was this oil not sold for three hundred days' wages and given to the poor?'"

(John 12:4–5)

It is Mary's extravagance that draws Judas's scorn. We are often generous with ourselves, rewarding ourselves with treats and favors. Yet, it is an entirely different matter when someone chooses to be generous with others. The perfumed oil Mary used to anoint the feet of Jesus was made from genuine aromatic nard, costing as much as an entire year's wages. And here is Mary, pouring it all out on someone's feet! A year's salary put away with interest could do much at the age of sixty-five. A year's salary spent on someone who would soon die! A year's wages used to anoint feet while poor people around her had empty stomachs! Mary's generosity cannot be understood apart from her deep love. Love gives; self takes.

In my forty-seven years as a pastor, I've witnessed countless examples of giving and taking—enough to fill an encyclopedia. Here's a true story: A single mom, who worked tirelessly as a nurse, brought dinner every single day for eight years to a neighbor who claimed to have no family and lived in poverty. She took days off work to drive him to doctor's appointments and even mowed his lawn. The nurse never once saw a visitor at the man's home. This woman, who had four young children and never received a penny in child support from her alcoholic ex-husband, never asked for or received any remuneration for the rides, meals, or lawn care. After the man's death, it was revealed that a niece, who lived in the same city, inherited his million-dollar estate!

Mary loved Jesus. Generosity is love in action. It isn't about money; it's about connection. It's about extending my heart and joining it with yours. It means sharing personal feelings, dreams, and time—not just physical things that can be stored away. Generosity means remembering someone's birthday or anniversary and sending them a card or making a phone call—not because you have to, but because you truly care. Christian love doesn't keep score or measure acts of generosity against the recipient's behavior. Words like freehearted, bounteous, and bighearted accompany the generous hand. And the truth is, it simply makes us happier when we give.

Returning to the story of the nurse: After the neighbor's death and the reading of his will, I asked her if she felt bitter about the fact that the old man had misrepresented his situation and taken advantage of her kindness. Not at all, she replied. She pointed to God's blessings: her Catholic faith, healthy kids, a good job, and her own large, loving family. She wasn't measuring her gifts by what the old man could provide but by how God had already provided for her. She could only feel sad for the old man—he had missed out on the joy of true connection and love.

Viktor E. Frankl once said, "The more one forgets himself—by giving himself to a cause to serve or another to love—the more human he is." This nurse's story reminds us that true generosity doesn't depend on the response or reward from others, but on the richness of our own hearts. As Jesus taught, *"Give and gifts will be given to you; a good measure, packed together, shaken down, and overflowing, will be poured into your lap. For the measure with which you measure will in return be measured out to you"* (Luke 6:38).

When we give, we reflect the love of Christ, who gave everything for us. Let us strive to be generous in all things, knowing that in doing so, we draw closer to the heart of God. In this spirit of giving, we find not only happiness but a deep and abiding sense of purpose and fulfillment. As we give freely, we become more fully human, more fully alive, and more fully in communion with the God who has given us everything.

Lenten Reflection: How have you been extravagantly generous to others? Who might you reach out to this Easter?

Day 42
Tuesday of Holy Week

April 15, 2025

Isaiah 49:1–6

Psalm 71:1–6, 15, 17

John 13:21–33, 36–38

Jesus said to Judas, "What you are going to do, do quickly."

(John 13:27)

Jesus is having dinner with two people who, within twenty-four hours, are going to betray Him: Judas and Peter. What is remarkable in this scene is that, despite knowing their imminent betrayal, Jesus's behavior remains kind, generous, and loving. In the customs of the time, it was an honor for a host to personally offer a piece of food to a guest at the table. Jesus extends this honor to Judas, reaching out to him in a final gesture of love and respect, right up to the last moment they share together. Similarly, by engaging in conversation and fellowship with Peter during the meal, Jesus offers him friendship, even knowing Peter's forthcoming denial. Jesus's love and kindness are not dependent on what others have done or might do. Even in the face of the most personal and painful betrayal—a kiss from

144

Judas—Jesus responds not with condemnation, but with a poignant observation.

This powerful demonstration of love teaches us that Jesus's love for us does not hinge on our behavior. He loves us and welcomes us to His table regardless of our imperfections. His love is steadfast and unwavering. If we waited until we were perfect to approach Communion, would any of us ever be able to partake? How is it that we might look down on another congregant approaching Communion, judging them for their behavior? Are we not called to leave the judging to Jesus? Just as Jesus spoke of being glorified at the Last Supper, so too are we glorified when we imitate His behavior. The Holy Spirit lives within us when we choose to live, act, and speak in love—independent of another's actions. It's easy to be kind to those who are kind to us; but as Christians, we are called to be kind, generous, and loving regardless. Living like Christ is how we share in His glory.

In every situation, with every person, a Christian is called to choose kindness, generosity, peace, civility, openness, and honesty. Jesus may have lost control over where He would go and what would happen to Him, but He never lost control over His own behavior. He remained steadfast, embodying the titles given to Him: King Jesus (John 19:3), Mighty God, Wonderful Counselor, Everlasting Father, Prince of Peace (Isaiah 9:6–7).

As we reflect on this, let us be encouraged to follow Jesus's example. No matter the circumstances or how others may treat us, we have the power to choose love, to extend grace, and to act with integrity. When we do so, we are not only following Christ's example—we are living out our true calling as His disciples. In every act of love, we are glorified with Him. Let us embrace this calling with joy and confidence, knowing that in choosing love, we reflect the very heart of God to the world around us.

Lenten Reflection: Have we refused to be with people because of their politics, criminal history, or public scandal? Has the Spirit always governed our behavior? How might we live in the Spirit that filled Jesus?

Day 43

Wednesday of Holy Week

April 16, 2025

Isaiah 50:4–9

Psalm 69:8–10, 21–22, 31, 33–34

Matthew 26:14–25

"Then Judas, his betrayer, seeing that Jesus had been condemned, deeply regretted what he had done. . ." *[He said,]* *"'I have sinned in betraying innocent blood' . . . Flinging the money into the temple, he departed and went off and hanged himself."*

(Matthew 27:3–5)

Judas committed suicide. If there was ever a time to address suicide, it should be Holy Week, for in Judas we see the most famous suicide of all time. It's easy to judge and dismiss Judas as greedy or ambitious, but the truth is, we don't really know what he was thinking. Perhaps he believed fully in Jesus's divinity and thought his actions might force Jesus to begin a campaign to overthrow the Romans. No one can truly know his motives. What we do know is that Judas couldn't face his friends after his betrayal. He was most likely ashamed of what he had done and traumatized by the consequences—seeing the scourging and impending crucifixion of his friend. To commit suicide, one must be in an incredibly dark place, having lost all hope. But do we truly believe that Judas is in hell? Do we think Jesus, who called Judas friend, would allow him to burn for eternity because of one tragic mistake?

I know what I believe. I believe in God's mercy. We even have a special Sunday to celebrate it—Divine Mercy Sunday. Mercy, by its very nature, is not justice. Justice is when you give people what they deserve. Justice is when a sentence is served fully, with no leniency. Justice, in its harshest form, would condemn someone to hell forever. But that's not mercy. Mercy is when compassion overrides justice, when forgiveness is extended even when justice demands retribution.

Jesus asks, *"If you then, who are wicked, know how to give good gifts to your children, how much more will your heavenly Father give good things to those who ask him"* (Matthew 7:11). The question is rhetorical because everyone understands the depth of a parent's love for their child. A parent would endure anything in place of their child. That is exactly the point Jesus is making. His love for us exceeds even the greatest love a human parent could have. I believe in the divine love of Jesus Christ. More than that, I believe Jesus is love incarnate. I believe that no parent of a child who commits suicide needs to lose one hour of sleep worrying about the eternal salvation of their child. Why? Because Jesus loves your child more than you do. If this is true—and it is true by the Lord's own words—then Jesus, who is love itself, would rather bear the pain Himself than allow your son or daughter to suffer any more than they already have.

When there is a suicide, I honestly don't feel the need to pray for the dead because I believe God was there to catch them when they fell. They may have expected darkness, but they found compassion instead. No, when there is a suicide, I pray for the living—that they may find comfort and healing in the arms of our merciful Lord.

So, let us hold onto the truth of God's boundless mercy. In our darkest moments and in the depths of our despair, God's love is there, reaching out to us. Let us trust that, no matter what, Jesus's love and mercy are greater than our failures and our fears. May this Holy Week remind us all that Christ's sacrifice was made out of love for each of us, and that love is stronger than death, stronger than despair, and strong enough to carry us through the darkest of times. We are never beyond the reach of God's mercy. We are always, always held in His love.

Lenten Reflection: Have you ever resented people getting parole after having committed some heinous crime? Do you forgive those who injure you personally? Consider opening your heart to divine mercy.

Day 44
Holy Thursday

April 17, 20

Exodus 12:1–8, 11–14 1
Corinthians 11:23–26
John 13:1–15

This is the night of Passover, and Jesus has gathered with His disciples to celebrate the traditional Jewish feast. He will humble Himself by getting down on the floor to wash their feet, modeling the posture of a servant that He expects from all who would follow Him. He takes the traditional bread and wine of Passover and transforms them into His Body and Blood. On this sacred night, the first priesthood is instituted as He commands that these actions be repeated in His memory. In the Garden of Gethsemane, He prays that this cup might pass from Him, yet He fully surrenders to God's will. It is on this night that the Lord is betrayed with a kiss.

As you witness these events unfold before you in your churches tonight, remember that we are not merely reenacting historical events from the past. In liturgy, the past is made present. This concept, foreign to most modern languages, transcends the simple boundaries of past, present, and future. In liturgy, time is not linear. We are not just remembering the Last Supper or duplicating the actions of Jesus as He takes the bread and wine in His hands and speaks the words of consecration. We believe that we are present with Jesus at the original Last Supper—the past is made present in a living, dynamic way.

To fully grasp this, one would need to understand Aramaic as it was spoken in the first century, a task beyond the scope of these meditations. However, it's important to recognize that our understanding of Holy Thursday is not a medieval invention but is rooted in the Jewish traditions of the first century. Even today, Jews do not simply reenact the Passover from Egypt. At the seder, they enter a sacred space where the past is made present, standing in solidarity with Jews of all time as they personally witness their liberation from Egypt.

Jesus knew exactly what He was doing when He chose this Passover night to institute the Sacrifice of the Mass. The gift of the Eucharist is not something to be taken lightly. Through Holy Communion, human beings come closer to God than at any other time. This is the most intimate connection we can have with the divine.

As you participate in these sacred events, open your mind, heart, and spirit to Jesus. Get down beside Him as He washes feet and wipes them dry. Sit with Him at the supper table as He offers His Body and Blood to the Father. Pray with Him in the garden. Feel the scourging on your back, the crown of thorns pressing into your head, and the humiliation of standing before a crowd that despises you. But remember, Jesus does not endure all of this for a stranger—He does it for you. He calls you His friend.

Let this Holy Thursday be a profound moment of encounter with the living Christ. Allow the reality of His sacrifice and His love for you to transform your heart. As you walk with Him through these sacred mysteries, may you draw ever closer to Him, knowing that in every act of humility, service, and love, Jesus is inviting you to share in His divine life. Embrace this invitation, and let it fill you with hope, peace, and the deep joy of being called a friend of the Savior.

Lenten Reflection: Jesus asked his disciples to "watch and pray that you may not undergo the test" (Matthew 26:41). Jesus is in Gethsemane and prison tonight. Churches are open so you might watch and pray with the Lord. Consider giving the Lord some time in prayer before the Blessed Sacrament.

Day 45
Good Friday

April 18, 2025

Isaiah 52:13–53:12

Hebrews 4:14–16; 5:7–9

John 18:1–19:42

Mel Gibson's *The Passion of the Christ* was a box office hit, but it diverges significantly from the way Scripture presents the crucifixion. While the movie is filled with graphic details of blood and gore, the Bible summarizes these events in just a few lines. John tells us simply, "Pilate took Jesus and had him scourged" (John 19:1). *"The soldiers wove a crown out of thorns and placed it on his head, and clothed him in a purple cloak"* (John 19:2). *"So they took Jesus, and carrying the cross himself he went out to what is called the Place of the Skull"* (John 19:16–17). While it's natural to try to reconcile the historical reality of scourging and crucifixion with the cinematic portrayal, Scripture does not dwell on these details.

Instead, the Bible directs our focus to the love that drove Jesus to the Cross, not the physical suffering. God's love for us is so immense that He was willing to die for us: *"No one has greater love than this, to lay down one's life for one's friends"* (John 15:13). The Cross represents all the senseless, ugly, horrific suffering in the world—it's the child who dies before ever speaking a word, the countless innocents lost in the futility of war, the deep emotional wounds within families, and the injustices that trap the poor. The Cross reminds us that our Creator does not stand apart as a distant bystander; instead, He shares in our pain.

The Passion of the Christ begins in the Garden of Gethsemane and concludes with Jesus's final breath on the Cross. This is the hour that He both prophesied and dreaded, the moment of His ultimate sacrifice. But the passion of these hours encompasses more than just pain and suffering; the word "passion" also means love—an intense, all-consuming love, like that between two people deeply drawn to each other. God watched His only Son die and yet remained patient and merciful, proving that love truly *"bears all things, believes all things, hopes all things, endures all things. Love never fails"* (1 Corinthians 13:7–8a).

Throughout His passion, Jesus embodies love and forgiveness. When the soldiers come to arrest Him, He commands Peter to lay down his sword. He offers understanding to Pilate, saying, *"You would have no power over me if it were not given to you from above"* (John 19:11). He forgives the soldiers, promises the repentant thief paradise, and even in His final moments, ensures His mother is cared for. He never retaliates, never speaks a harsh word. Against the darkest cruelty and evil, He shines as a blazing fire of love. Christ's Passion is, above all, a story of love—love that overshadows suffering.

As Jesus hangs on the Cross, He says, *"I thirst"* (John 19:28). But His thirst is not only physical; it reflects our own unquenchable need for answers, for meaning. Jesus, the Water of Life, comes to satisfy this deepest of thirsts. He is the answer to why we are here, the purpose of our lives. Without Him, we would all fall back into dust, into the nothingness from which we came. In Jesus, God thirsts for a response from His creation, a desire for relationship, love, and communion. And yet, humanity responds with a cross. We say, "No." And with that, Jesus gives up His Spirit and dies.

It should have been the end of our story, but even after all this, Jesus does not give up on us. He rises from the dead, repaying evil with good, curses with blessings, and death with life. It is called Good Friday not because of what we did, but because of what He did. He is love crucified, our Savior, and our Redeemer.

As we reflect on these sacred events, let us hold onto the truth that no matter the darkness, no matter the suffering, love will always have the final word. Jesus's sacrifice was not just an act of suffering but the ultimate expression of divine love. In His resurrection, we find hope, renewal, and the promise of new life. Let this Good Friday be a reminder that through Christ's love, all things are made new. We are not abandoned; we are redeemed. And in that redemption, we find our hope, our strength, and our peace.

Lenten Reflection: Jesus says "I thirst" directly to you. What can you offer him?

Day 46

Holy Saturday/Easter Vigil

April 19, 2025

(1 of 7) Genesis 1:1–2:2

Romans 6:3–11

Luke 24:1–12

Tonight's Vigil is the mother of all liturgies, the pinnacle of the Church's celebration. Mass begins in total darkness, symbolizing the void before creation. At the entrance to the church, the priest lights a new fire, a powerful symbol of God's first creative act: light. From this new fire, the Paschal candle, representing Christ the Light, is lit. This candle, etched with sacred symbols, recalls the pillar of fire that guided the Israelites through the Red Sea. As it moves slowly through the center aisle toward the sanctuary, the chant of "Christ our Light" echoes through the church, and congregants light their own candles. This spreading light represents the Spirit moving over the earth as the Gospel was preached and souls were welcomed into the Body of Christ, the Church.

As the Paschal candle enters the sanctuary, the Exsultet is chanted, a hymn of praise that has its roots in the court of Charlemagne over 1,200 years ago. This ancient hymn recounts salvation history, tracing God's deliverance of His people from Egypt to the waters of Baptism. It proclaims that Christ has dispelled the darkness of sin and death, bringing us into the light of eternal life.

Following the Exsultet, seven Bible readings trace God's mighty works throughout history, leading to the climax of His plan in the birth, death, and resurrection of Jesus Christ. Each reading is a reminder of God's unwavering faithfulness and His desire to bring us into communion with Him.

On this sacred night, those who have prepared all year for reception into the Church receive the sacraments of Baptism and Confirmation. Through these sacraments, they are welcomed into the fullness of life in Christ. The Vigil then culminates in the celebration of the Eucharist, where Christ becomes truly present in flesh and blood. In this moment of profound intimacy, our communion with the Father is made complete as Christ now dwells within us, both physically and spiritually. The God who once dwelled in the Holy of Holies within the Jerusalem Temple now enters our very bodies, making us temples of the Holy Spirit. During this Vigil, we celebrate the incredible mystery of God entering time and space so that He might gather us into His loving arms and grant us eternal life. As Jesus Himself said, *"I am the living bread that came down from heaven; whoever eats this bread will live forever; and the bread that I will give is my flesh for the life of the world"* (John 6:51).

The Liturgy is long, and in our fast-paced, modern world, we are often unaccustomed to resting in God's presence, allowing the Holy Spirit to carry us and renew us. But if we could only pause our rush to nowhere and open ourselves to the stillness and depth of God's presence, this ancient liturgy could work its wonder, breathing new life into our weary spirits.

Tonight, as we gather in the darkness and witness the light of Christ filling the sanctuary, let us allow that light to fill our hearts as well. Let us embrace the fullness of this sacred night, knowing that in these moments, heaven and earth touch, and we are drawn into the eternal love of God. As we leave this Vigil, may we carry the light of Christ within us, shining brightly in the world, and may the wonder of this night continue to renew and strengthen us in our journey of faith. Christ is risen, and through Him, we are made new! Alleluia!

Easter Reflection: Consider participating in this year's Easter Vigil, if not in person, then via the internet or television. Jump into God's arms and see where the Spirit takes you!

Day 47

Easter Sunday

April 20, 2025

(1ˢᵗ) Acts 10:34a, 37–43

(2ⁿᵈ) Colossians 3:1–4 or 1 Corinthians 5:6b–8

(3ʳᵈ) John 20:1–9 or Matthew 28:1–10

Finally, Jesus is delivered into the hands of women! All four Gospels note that it was women who went to the tomb to anoint the body of Jesus. Men conspired against Him, betrayed Him, denied Him, judged, and executed Him. Yet, in death, Jesus falls into the arms of His mother, ending His earthly life where He began it—in the embrace and care of a woman. While men stayed away from dead bodies, it was the women who washed and anointed them. And it was a woman who first encountered the resurrected Christ and announced the Good News. It raises an honest and reasonable question: why can't women proclaim this same news in Catholic worship today?

Mary at the empty tomb, John hearing the news for the first time, and later, John recognizing Christ as a stranger on the shore—these moments are not coincidences. Those who love Jesus deeply are often the first to recognize His presence. As you read these reflections, it is with the hope of deepening your love for Jesus. And as that love grows, you can expect to see Him more clearly in your life. He will come to you! Just as the Father took the dead body of Jesus and transformed it into a glorified Body, the Spirit is at work in you now. Something is happening within your heart, mind, body, and soul. The Kingdom of God is drawing near to you, thinning the boundary between the material world and the spiritual realm. Angels cross over. Saints speak. Hearts are moved. Peace begins to flow. Can you feel it? Something wonderful is happening! Your love, like that of Mary and John, is creating something new and beautiful.

"Mary of Magdala went and announced to the disciples, 'I have seen the Lord'" (John 20:18). This is the proclamation we are called to make as well. We must be people who embrace the truth of Christ and allow the Spirit to work through us. Just as Jesus was faithful to God and was raised from the dead, so too will your faithfulness be rewarded. You may have suffered loss—the loss of work, health, or love. You may have witnessed death— the death of a dream, a relationship, a promise, or even a child. But God will not let you bear this burden alone. The Spirit is not just a distant promise; it is a living reality within you right now. Take away the stone, and let the Spirit transform your life.

We often treat Easter as just another program on television, something to watch passively from our

161

chairs. But the resurrection is not a make-believe story. Christ is not a fictional character. He is real! He is risen, and He is with you now! See the risen Jesus who walks beside you and, like Mary, proclaim, *"I have seen the Lord."*

Speak His name out loud: Jesus. *"The name that is above every name, that at the name of Jesus every knee should bend, of those in heaven and on earth and under the earth, and every tongue confess that Jesus Christ is Lord, to the glory of God the Father"* (Philippians 2:9b–11).

In a world filled with unspeakable suffering, senseless violence, and the death of innocence, we are no longer mere observers. The daily news spills over us from our devices, weighing us down with the horrors of what we see around us. This is a time when the light of Jesus is needed more than ever, a time of growing darkness and unbelief. Christ needs you to be His light. He needs you to bear witness to His Good News, to share the gift of the Spirit, and to proclaim the promise of transformation and new life. The world is waiting to hear the news of Jesus's resurrection. You, anointed, predestined, chosen—you are called to deliver it! Christ is risen. Alleluia! Alleluia!

---

[i] Brian Tracy
[ii] Winston Churchill

Made in the USA
Coppell, TX
28 January 2025

45129666R00100